Totally Bound Publishin

Singl
The G
From a Lady ...

ELLIE'S RULES

CASSIE O'BRIEN

ELLIE'S RULES

Dedication

'Absent Friends' — with my love.

Chapter One

I stretched as I woke and shook the shoulder of the man asleep beside me when I glanced at the digital display of the bedside clock.

"Mark, wake up. It's time you went home before anyone else is up and sees you leave my hotel room."

I pressed the bedhead switch and turned on the wall-mounted lights. Mark grunted and burrowed his face into the pillow, so all I could see of him was his dark-blond, sleep-tussled hair. I pushed the duvet off us and smacked his up-turned arse cheek. "Awake, you. *Now.*"

He turned his head to the side and opened one eye. "You wouldn't like to do that again, would you? I think I rather liked it…"

I slapped his butt once more. "Maybe next time, but for now, get yourself out of here."

He rolled onto his back, his cock stiffening. "You're quite sure you wouldn't like a little more?"

My pussy dampened at the sight, but I ignored my arousal and pointed toward my bedroom door. "Out, you greedy bugger."

He swung his legs off the bed with a still-sleepy smile. "But that's what you like about me."

I straightened the duvet over my legs as he took his clothes out of the wardrobe and watched his cock disappear inside the snug fit of his boxer shorts.

"So I do, but not the prospect of a whisper of undue influence leaking out into the ether because one of my work colleagues has happened to spot you leaving my room."

Mark pulled on his trousers, tucked in his shirt and fastened his zipper then leaned over the bed and kissed me, his lips soft on my cheek. "Okay, my little she-dragon. I'm out of here. Are you going to be kind to me later?"

"Nope." I yawned. "I'll be fair and impartial as always, but the best interests of the regulatory authority I represent will always guide my final decision."

He sighed and picked up his suit jacket. "I should know better than to expect any other answer from you, but you can't blame a man for living in hope."

I turned my face to my pillow. "As I live in hope you'll shut the door behind you quietly on your way out. See you at ten."

He walked to my hotel room door and looked over his shoulder as he opened it. "Ellie McAllister, you're going to kill me at the meeting, aren't you?"

I lifted my head. "No, Mr. Walker. It won't quite be a knife to the jugular unless I re-read your proposal over breakfast and change my mind because I haven't managed to catch a couple of extra hours of looked-for sleep. Easy on that door now, when you shut it."

Mark smiled and eased the door into its latch as he left. I darkened the room again, closed my eyes and slept until my phone alarm sounded at seven-thirty, then showered, made up my face with a pale, minimal look and dressed in a dark, knee-length business skirt-suit, a white, buttoned-to-the-neck shirt and three-inch heels to bring my five-foot-eight height up nearer average man-level. I finished by scraping my hair back from my face and twisting the length of it into a bun secured by an old-fashioned hair net on the nape of my neck, then added 'geek' spectacles of zero magnification.

My attaché case and overnight bag in hand, I exited my hotel room and rode the lift down to the restaurant to see my two colleagues already seated—Joanne, a legal exec, and Leza, an admin assistant. I sat and asked, "Did you sleep well? Is everything good to go?"

Joanne nodded. "I did, thanks, then had the pool to myself when I took an early swim around six. I re-read the brief before I came down for breakfast and your response is appropriate to the proposal. If they're expecting our immediate approval, they're living in la-la land, but I don't get that expectation from the wording of it."

Leza smiled. "I'll take the minutes on my tablet. I've typed up and printed the formalities, short as they are."

The waiter hovered and we gave him our order for the lighter breakfast option—thinly sliced smoked salmon with brown bread and butter, black tea and a sharing platter of fresh fruit.

Leza looked at her plate when he brought our order to the table and set the food in front of us. "It's good to get out of the office sometimes, isn't it? I wouldn't normally bother with breakfast on a work day other than perhaps a chocolate bar to eat on the train."

Joanne smiled and cut into her smoked salmon. "It's just a shame the glass of champagne that should accompany this is off limits."

Leza sighed. "Mm-m… I could go for that. Smoked salmon and champagne."

I popped the latches on my attaché case, took three copies of my official reply to Mark's proposal out of it and passed two of them over. Leza looked at the cover page of her copy, traced her fingertip under his name and added, "Preferably after a night rolling around in bed with Mark Walker with the hope of a second helping of him to come after breakfast."

Joanne laughed. "In your dreams. I happen to know Julie Summers dropped a couple of more-than-obvious hints his way and he didn't go for them, so I don't think any of us sitting around this table stand a chance of getting our hands on him."

"He didn't fancy Julie Summers? Wow," Leza said. "But would it break the rules to date him, Jo?"

"Technically, no," Joanne told her, "so long as you declared your involvement with him on the personal interests register, but you'd have to stop working on anything to do with his company and that wouldn't go down well with those higher up the career chain. You'd probably find yourself relegated to the sidelines with any hope trashed that you held for future promotion."

I pushed my glasses higher up my nose as Joanne's words sent a shiver down my back, although my groin, alive with the kind of tremor that wanted more of what Mark had done to my body in the night, ignored her warning. I cleared my throat and sat a little straighter.

"Stow the daydreams, ladies. We're about to head to a business meeting with him. Eyes down and enjoy your breakfast. We have a job to do."

I turned the cover page of my copy and read as I ate. Joanne flicked to the last page on hers and looked at me over the top of her fork. "What will you do if the independent audit firm he selects is the 'rather too close to home' bunch that rent offices in the same building as his?"

I put my cutlery on my plate and placed my paperwork back in my case. "There's nothing I can do. The choice is his. I'll try to emphasize the word *independent*, to hint that the audit firm you eat lunch with every day is okay to sign off your year-end accounts but probably not the best choice if what you're after is regulatory approval for a business model that's never been trialed before."

"Given the loophole you've picked up, it shouldn't come as much of a surprise to him that we're going to be a little fussy over this," Joanne said.

I shrugged, pushed my plate away and stood. "I've no suspicion of intent to exploit from my monitoring of the company's previous financial transactions, but the potential's there to asset-strip the profitable policies and dump the rest. Go on ahead of me after the meeting. I'll stay behind and drop a hint in his ear about the precedence. Let's get to it, ladies."

Joanne and Leza followed me out of the restaurant. We deposited our overnight bags with reception and I settled our bill then pocketed the receipt for the allowable portion to add to my month's expenses claim. The hotel was only a brisk walk away from Mark's offices and Joanne swung open the door to the reception area of Walker and Timpson Asset Management Limited ten minutes later. I gave our names at the welcome desk and twenty minutes after that, courtesies of hand-shaking completed and offers of coffee and water turned down, I sat at the conference table with Joanne and Leza, one to each side of me, and faced Mark, along with the two of his work colleagues who accompanied him. I opened my attaché case, took my written conclusion out of it and looked at him. "Are you happy for Leza to take the minutes or would you prefer one of your staff to do so?"

"Leza's fine." Mark smiled.

I did not reciprocate, a smile being something never seen on my face during a business meeting, with Mark or anyone else. I turned to Leza, who was tapping on her tablet screen. "You have the names of those present?"

She nodded. "Sure. Ready to go when you are."

I picked up my script. "I'll give you my decision straight through. There are no points of discussion in it." I dropped my gaze and began.

"I have reviewed the business proposal received from you, Walker and Timpson, along with your financial statements, and I have two areas of concern that need to be addressed before this scheme can be further considered for regulatory approval. The first is the safeguarding of vulnerable policyholders, namely those whose 'premium paid' falls short of the expected 'settlement due' in the event of their making a valid claim. The second is the limited liability status of Walker and Timpson. With these concerns in mind, I would require a full all-area audit to be completed by an external firm of accountants of your choice" — I paused and looked up from my script into the faces in front of me — "with the proviso that the accounting firm selected should be *fully* independent of this company. On my review of the audit data, your proposal will be re-examined. A hard copy of this decision will be left with you and also published on our online information portal at such time as I deem it appropriate to do so. The minutes of this meeting will be emailed to you."

I put my script onto the table and withdrew my attention against any attempt to involve me in a discussion that might lead to the sin of sins — a regulator defending or justifying their decision. Joanne sat straighter, ready to deal with any objection or counter-argument on my behalf, but none came.

"That concludes our business," she said.

"We'll give your decision our attention over the next few days," Mark replied, with a noticeable absence of a smile.

The men on the other side of the table pushed their chairs back and stood. I picked up my case, opened it and flicked through the contents, looking for nothing really at all. Leza flipped the cover of her tablet shut and followed Joanne and Mark's colleagues out of the room. I closed my case, looked at Mark's still unsmiling face and actually committed the sin of sins as I asked, "So, what were you expecting?"

Mark retook his seat and faced me with a stiffness to his shoulders that told me he'd taken the wording of my decision personally. "Whatever else I expected, it was not that as a matter of public record it would be implied that I may be intending to front-load the profitable policies and sink the remainder."

I gazed at the crease of a frown between his eyes then committed the most cardinal sin of all and explained.

"Mark, the search for exploitable loopholes is my brief. Making a judgement call on whether the company concerned would use them is not. I find them. I deal with them. I fully expect your audit results to be squeaky clean. You'll get your approval if so, and if your new business model works as you predict, your company will make its oodles of cash. Your business model will then be copied by other companies eager for a slice of the pie and they won't all be as scrupulous as you."

"You've used us to set precedent?"

"Sorry, but not sorry, yes. The temptation to assign the unprofitable polices to a shell subsidiary company of limited liability then fold that company at a loss of only fifty quid will be too much to resist for some of the businesses that will jump on your bandwagon. If I approve your scheme, I'll retrospectively publish this decision, because it has to be known that we're aware of the possibility of it happening. And with my apologies to the audit company you use, you share office facilities with them—the loos, lunch venues—and you probably all mingle in the wine bar on the ground floor on Friday evenings. My message on that front is directed at any company that may think they can sneak a 'friend of a friend' audit past us."

His shoulders relaxed. "Okay. Point taken. Although I can assure you we don't mingle in a work-related way with our auditors any more than I'm about to rip off little old ladies with their five-pounds-a-month policies that pay out fifty times that every time they so much as break a fingernail."

I stood and picked up my case. "As I'm rather banking on, being as it will be my name on the dotted line that signs off on the final approval. If this goes tits-up, it takes me down with it. I'll wait to hear from you."

I shut the door behind me to the sound of his voice. "It won't—"

I rode the lift down and handed back my visitor badge at the welcome desk. Joanne and Leza waited for me beside it. I looked at the time on my phone. "There's a train departing for London just after the hour. If we quick-walk, we can just about make it."

Joanne nodded and stepped up the pace. We retrieved our overnight bags from the hotel, hot-footed it through town to the station and jumped onto the train with two minutes to spare. Leza, red-faced, spluttered as we found seats for four, two on each side of a central table. "Jesus, I'm puffed."

Joanne, gym-honed and barely winded like me, laughed. "Look at the state of you! And you thought you could go several rounds in the sack with the super-fit Mark Walker? No chance!"

"I'd give it a damn good shot." Leza wheezed to Joanne's snort. I looked at Joanne sitting beside me then at Leza sat opposite her, and cleared my throat to call them to order.

"Enough, ladies. Thank you."

"Sorry, Ellie," Joanne said. "That was inappropriate. How did your hint about the precedence go down?"

I squeezed my knees together against my own inappropriate thoughts of the feel of Mark's mouth sucking between my legs and shortened the extent of our conversation. "Initially not happy, but with a couple of pointed remarks, it was message received."

"Good." Joanne smiled.

Leza leaned back and took her e-reader out of her bag as my phone vibrated. Joanne glanced at the screen as it lit up with the name calling — Jaydon Scott, the dark-haired elder brother of Lucy, the captain of the football team I played for. I accepted the call but kept my answers minimal to match the straight-laced reputation I cultivated at work. "Jay. Hi."

"Are you still up for drinks at Lucy's tonight?"

"I'll be there."

"Shall I swing by your place so we can walk over together?"

Having a pretty good idea of what Jay would really like to swing by mine for but unsure it was a road I wished to go down with my skin still tingling from my night in bed with Mark, I sidestepped his offer. "I'm out of the office on business today. Best if I make my own way, I think."

"Oh, okay. But you're definitely coming?"

"Sure. See you later."

I cut the call to Joanne's look of enquiry. "Your boyfriend?"

"Not as such." I shrugged. "He's a nice guy, but I'm not much into the dating thing."

"That's a shame…if he's nice."

I shrugged again, retrieved my laptop from my attaché case then loaded up a spreadsheet and further sealed my reputation as the office's least interesting female by getting on with some work without any other comment on the subject. The train pulled into London Bridge station in time for us to take a late lunch break. Leza headed to McDonald's, Joanne to Pret's, while I walked on to the office, bought a sandwich from the local snack bar then worked through until six and let myself into my hard-saved-for studio flat a few minutes after seven. My front door opened directly onto an all-purpose living area with a kitchenette and, above it, a half-mezzanine bedroom accompanied by a walk-in en suite wet room — all of it my prized little-bit-of-London space that had taken three years of scrimping to accumulate a down payment that elsewhere in the country would have allowed me to purchase the flat outright.

I put my attaché case beside the sofa, took my overnight bag to my bedroom then showered, put on my wrap and walked downstairs to inspect the interior of my fridge. The sparse contents that greeted me forewarned of a supermarket trip in the morning, but with Lucy providing hot snacks later, I only wanted the bottle of cold beer on the shelf. I flicked the television on, chose a music channel then sat on the sofa and contemplated the evening that could end with Jay in my bed. As I sipped, the track changed to Queen's *Play the Game* and the opening lyrics scrolling across the bottom of the screen brought to mind my time in bed with Mark.

I smiled as I remembered how our occasional nights together had begun—at an afternoon seminar for which the conference room of a London hotel had been booked for a PR undertaking on behalf of Her Majesty's government. Speakers, including me, were attending to try to convince an audience of invited guests that our various tax-raising or regulatory departments weren't really mad, bad and only in existence to piss them off.

The seminar reached its early evening wine and nibbles finale. I stood my wine glass on a table as I finished a round of polite nothings with a rather pompous accountant from Reading and headed for the hotel lobby and the ladies' loo. A corner bar caught my eye when I exited the Ladies and I walked toward it to buy a gin and tonic in preference to another glass of complimentary, but government-priced, wine. I took a healthy swallow after the barman poured and heard Mark's voice as I replaced my debit card into its allocated slot and dropped my purse into my jacket pocket.

"Tut, tut, Ms. McAllister. Sneaking out to the bar whilst still on duty. Is that allowed?"

I picked up my glass and felt the tummy tickle that the sight or sound of Mark always gave me, looked around and saw him standing in the far corner of the bar holding a glass half-full of a drink similar to mine. I raised my glass, toasted him then drank another mouthful.

"Not just allowed but necessary. The only antidote to that well-known disease 'seminar rigor mortis' – something I see you seem to have caught a dose of yourself."

Mark smiled. "Are you allowed to drink your drink with me outside of the conference room or would that be counted as fraternizing with the enemy?"

I pushed my spectacles down my nose a little and looked at him over their top. "Now, Mr. Walker, have I not just spent a half-hour telling you what a delightful, sweet, caring bunch we regulators are? I used pictures and everything. I'm sure one of them even assured you of our offer of friendly advice, should you need it."

He laughed and my stomach gave me another jolt. "I'd rather stick my hand into a tankful of piranhas, thanks."

I walked around to his side of the bar and smiled. "A wise choice."

He grinned. "Whoa. First a sense of humor and now she smiles. I'm not sure my surprise-o-meter can take the strain."

I obliged and smiled again. He finished his drink, looked at my glass and asked, "Another?"

I drank another mouthful and handed it to him. "Thanks."

The barman put our refreshed drinks in front of us. I sipped mine and asked, "What are you doing here, anyway? You could have stitched up one of your scurrying minions to attend in your place."

He chinked his glass on mine and caught my eye. I breathed in deeper as the blue of his irises did the 'Paul Newman' twinkly thing.

"You have to show willingness and attend one of these events at least once a year. I had a couple of meetings arranged in London for tomorrow, so I booked the hotel, accepted the invitation and will get to avoid the over-packed commuter train out of Brighton in the morning."

"Good call," I said.

"Why don't you, though? Smile at work? You look like you've just sucked on a lemon most of the time," he asked.

"Excellent." I smiled. "And my appearance suggests 'geek'?"

"Well, prudishly up her own arse, actually."

I laughed. "Oh, even better."

"Why?" He grinned.

I took a quick look around the bar. "Well, with an absence of my beloved work colleagues…" I sipped my drink. "After my degree and master's, I was recruited on HM gov's fast-track graduate entry program. I was promoted over the heads of a couple of long-servers during my first appointment and the whispers started. By the time the office had decided how many tutors and department heads I must have slept with to get where I was, I might as well have put both degrees in the bin. I moved sideways, became a regulator and created a persona who's been promoted ahead of her age because she's a serious-minded, un-fanciable geek."

"You could have registered a formal complaint," he countered.

I answered with a small shrug. "No, not for that. Sad but true. You register a formal complaint and no matter what the outcome is, the fact that you made a complaint at all follows you around from department to department like a bad smell."

He put his glass on the bar. "So, you're not a geek or…"

I looked into his eyes and my heart gave a double tap as I saw the glint of speculation in them. I finished his sentence for him with an ending of my own. "Or you could tell me your room number and find out."

"And you'd show up?" he asked.

"If you leave the bar first…"

He turned and murmured, "Twenty-one-thirty."

I watched him walk away and questioned my offer when he had gone. Reckless, for sure, but I was no more immune from wanting him than any other red-blooded female in the office, and a competitive spark of 'let's see what I can surprise you with next' made my decision for me. I sipped the end of my drink and gave him a ten-minute head start, then walked out of the bar in the direction of the hotel lifts.

Mark, sans his jacket and tie, opened his door to my knock and widened the gap to invite me in. "I wasn't sure you meant it."

I looked at the singular gin and tonic that stood on the hotel-generic small, round table with a chair to either side of it. "No, you weren't, were you? I'll drink yours while you pour another, shall I?"

He closed the door behind me and opened the mini-bar. I removed my glasses as he ducked his head to look into it, put them into my jacket pocket as I shrugged it off and pulled my bun net away from my hair. My hair tumbled down and over my shoulders. He turned toward me with a miniature spirit bottle in his hand and his eyes widened to his grin. "Okay. My surprise-o-meter has just gone into overload. How do you make that amount of hair disappear?"

"Practice." I dropped my jacket onto the dressing table stool, undid the first four buttons on my shirt and unlatched the front-fastening of the slightly-too-small sports bra I wore to ensure that the size and bounce of my breasts was not obvious. My bra parted and the fullness of my double-D-sized breasts sprang free to form a cleavage in the open V of my shirt.

Mark stared and my pussy grew damper at the intensity of his gaze. I retrieved my purse from my jacket, turned and sauntered toward the table, knowing that as unflattering as the length of my skirt was, it skimmed and moved over my butt cheeks as I walked without my suit jacket to obscure the view. I sat, put my purse on the table and picked up his glass. He poured his drink and sat in the chair opposite. "So, what do you like to do when you're not being a she-dragon at work?"

I sipped and looked at him. "I like to play competitive sports—golf in the summer, football in the winter then there's boxing…" I paused and vamped it up a notch. "And bed wrestling." I gazed into his eyes and saw no sign of a blue twinkle but a more predatory gleam. I put my drink on the table, dipped my fingers into my purse and took out a foil-covered square. "Want to play?"

His hardening erection pressed against the crotch of his trousers as he stood and unfastened his shirt. I gazed at his firm, smooth chest beneath wider shoulders and the packed muscles of his belly, stood and threw the condom to land on the bed as I kicked off my shoes then shrugged off my shirt and bra, unzipped my skirt and stepped out of it to stand naked, bar the merest wisp of lace covering my wet pussy. He toed off his shoes, unzipped his trousers and took them off with his boxers and socks. I gazed at his stiff cock and thought, Oh, fuck, yes.

I stepped out of my thong and back toward the bed. Mark matched my movement, urged me down onto it and fastened his mouth on mine, his hands on my shoulders. I nearly sighed, melting beneath him as he gave me all I'd ever wanted from a kiss, but I pulled away and bit his neck. He released his hold on me as he gasped. I twisted from beneath him, reversed our position then straddled him at his waist, pinned his shoulders and dangled my breast over his mouth. "Uh-uh. A little light on the hold there, I think."

He raised his head, drew my nipple into his mouth and I breathed deeper to the pull of his suck. I offered my other breast to his lips when he released the first. He reached to grasp it. I gripped his hands and held them then brushed his mouth with the hard nub of my nipple and teased. "You have to try harder than that."

He tilted his lips in the start of a smile. "Oh…do I?" He lifted his shoulders and tried to use his heavier weight to tip me onto my back. I moved quickly, grasped his hips, poised my mouth over his erection, licked up his shaft and sucked on his warm, sweet cockhead until his breathing deepened then released him. "Three-nil to me at the moment, I believe. I'm going to have your cum in my mouth before you've even fucked me, at this rate."

Mark used his weight with more purpose to turn and pin me to the bed. "Not before I've tasted you first." He fastened his mouth over my nipple and drew on it as greedily as I'd ever hoped for.

I dug my fingertips into his back. "Oh, good..."

I breathed deeper as he squeezed and sucked one breast then the other, panted as he held my hips and kissed down my body then licked and explored my pussy with his tongue. He lifted his head and reached for the condom. I reached it first, tore the packet open with my teeth and offered it to him. "An honorable draw on the foreplay, I think."

I parted my legs as he rolled on the condom. He lay over me, slid his finger through my wetness then inside me, added another, stroked and replaced them with his cock. I pushed my pelvis against his as he entered me and matched his thrusts, hip-to-hip, his cock pounding inside me until muscles tightened in my groin and I shouted out my climax in response to his fierce finale.

"Fuck! Yes!"

Mark tensed. His thrusts shorted to his orgasmic groan. He stilled, panting, and I held on tight around him until my heartbeat steadied, along with his breathing. He eased his cock out, dealt with the condom and turned onto his side. I lay on mine to face him.

He trailed his fingertips over the taut contours of my body from shoulder to hip. "So, certainly an athlete. Golf I get, but do you really play football and go to watch boxing?"

"Yep." I smiled. "I keep goal for Forest Hill Ladies and I don't go to bouts to sit ringside. I box in them. How about you?"

"Watersports for me." He smiled back. "It's why I live on the coast. Windsurfing mainly, but I'll take anything on the water if it has a sail, not a motor."

"Living in London and originally from the country, it's not something that's come my way."

"Give me a shout if you're down this way out of work time. I'll take you out on one of the sailing club's ketches."

I planted a quick kiss on his lips and swung my legs off the bed. "Given our work relationship, it's best if I don't. Better if we leave this as a for-one-day-only special offer..."

Which it hadn't been. I visited Mark's hotel room when he came to our office in London. He visited mine on the rarer occasions that government expenses allowed for an overnight stay, and neither of us discussed work on more than a superficial level in the bedroom or communicated about anything other than work outside of it.

Chapter Two

My phone vibrated and called a halt to my thoughts. I picked it up, saw the time was nearing nine and opened a message from Lucy.

Hiya. You okay? Jay's mixing some amazing Cosmopolitans and you're not here.

I pushed the pussy-tingling-but-career-hazardous Mark Walker out of my head and tapped back.

Sorry. I didn't get home until after seven. I'll be with you shortly.

Fantastic. See you soon.

I walked upstairs and dressed in jeans with a pretty satin bra beneath a long-sleeved ribbed top then made up my face with an evening but not night-on-the-town look. I stepped into chunky-heeled, calf-length boots and shrugged my hooded all-weather parka on then checked my purse for cash, cards and keys and added my phone.

The walk to Lucy's took me less than twenty minutes with my hood up against a late September drizzle and I rang the doorbell of her luxurious-for-London, two-up-two-down terraced house.

She opened the front door, grabbed my arm and pulled me inside with a squeal. "Yay! You're here! You're at least three cocktails behind the rest of us."

I put down my hood, unzipped my coat, walked through the narrow hallway to her sitting room and was gathered into a warm, hairy hug as I stepped through the door. I side-swiped Jay's arm. "Bear. Put me down. Your beard tickles."

He grinned as he did so. I looked into the brown eyes of the man that had been my weekend bed companion for the last couple of months and returned his smile. "So, what's this I've been hearing about your skill in mixing cocktails?"

"Coming right up," he said and reached for the vodka bottle standing on the dining table that had been set up for the evening as a wet bar. I took off my coat, draped it over the back of a chair and watched him pour a double measure of vodka, then one of Cointreau over ice in the shaker before adding a splash of cranberry juice and a small measure of soda water. "Blimey, Bear. That's lethal!"

He shook, strained the contents of the shaker into a martini glass and handed it over. "Yep, but they taste good."

I sipped and found the cocktail deceptively easy to drink, with the sweetness of orange Cointreau added to that of the cranberry. Lucy laughed loudly behind me. Our defender, Sarah, snorted and our center forward,

25

Cheryl, dissolved into giggles. I looked at Jay. "How many have they had?"

Jay's gaze followed mine. "That's the fourth. I think you're going to have your work cut out in goal tomorrow."

I toasted him with my glass and drank another mouthful. It slipped down without the slightest protest from the back of my throat. "Well, thank you for that...not."

He smiled. "Nah. You'll probably be fine. Lucy said you don't kick off until two."

I walked over to them, perched on the arm of the sofa and Sarah giggled.

"You'll love this one, Ellie. She's dumped Sean. Go on, Lucy. Gross Ellie out too!"

Lucy slurped her drink. "Well, he invited me to the opening bash of a swanky new wine bar in Soho. The Secret something or other it's called..." She paused, finished the end of her cocktail and waved her empty glass at Jay. He took it from her and caught my eye with a wink when he brought it back full. "So..." she continued, "there we were, dressed to the nines and he picked up a cocktail stick that someone had left beside an empty glass on the bar..." She snorted and pointed to her ear. "And swirled it around and around until he pulled it out with a lump of wax on the end of it, which he then examined in detail before rolling it into a ball and playing with it."

I winced. "Oh, shit! Ugh!"

"I can't tell you how quick I made my excuses and legged it!" Lucy snorted to Sarah's and Cheryl's renewed giggles.

"At a full sprint, I should think!" I laughed and stood. "Back in a min. I'll just get a refill."

I said hi to Cheryl's and Sarah's partners, Hugh and Dave, as I passed them, who were beating each other up by way of a game on the PlayStation, and handed my empty glass to Jay. "I'll stick with a gin and tonic, if you've got one."

"Sure," he said, mixed one and passed it to me. "I heard Lucy telling you about Sean. She always goes on a bit of bender after breaking up with someone."

"Yeah, I know. I was around when she and Dan parted company."

Jay frowned. "Now, that one was *bad*. There would have been wedding bells there if the pics of exactly what he was doing with that stripper on his mate's stag night hadn't hit Facebook."

Another loud burst of laughter sounded as Lucy stood, bumped into the arm of the sofa then nearly tripped over a chair as she wavered toward the kitchen. I raised my eyebrows at Jay and put my glass down. "I have a feeling you're going to be fully occupied on brotherly hair-holding toilet duty tonight."

He looked at Lucy. "Sorry, Ellie, but yeah, it looks like it."

I mouthed 'no worries' and followed Lucy to her kitchen. She blinked at the oven then stared as if she'd never seen one before. I opened it, saw trays of Chinese and Indian party food on the verge of being cooked too crispy, put on an oven glove and pulled them out. Plates waited on the work surface. I filled them, shooed Lucy back to her seat on the sofa then fetched the food from the kitchen and passed it around.

Jay took a couple of spring rolls from the last plate I brought out. "Thanks, Ellie. Left to our Lucy, this lot would have been either charcoal or all over the kitchen floor."

I handed him the plate, kissed his cheek just above his face fur and picked up my coat. "You'll probably wish it had been when it reappears again shortly. I arrived too late. I'm a bit out of sync tonight, so, no fuss, but I'll slip off home now."

Jay kissed me back. "I wish I could. It ain't going to be pretty. I'll see you tomorrow after the match?"

I nodded, walked down the hallway and let myself out of the front door. The drizzle had stopped, although the air still felt damp, so I pulled up my hood and saw that the hot chicken shop was still open as I turned the corner. The smell of fried food made my stomach grumble, so I stepped inside it, ordered a large portion of fries topped with melted cheese and ate them as I walked home.

* * * *

I woke at seven in the morning, happy not to have the hangover from hell, took my pill with my breakfast coffee and received a text from Lucy as I drank it.

Where did you get to? You lightweight!

I messaged her a row of halo-topped emojis.

How's your head?

Groan. Groan. But not as bad as it should be, being as the last couple of Cosmos ended up down the toilet pan. See you at the club at 1.

I laughed at my phone then headed out to refill my fridge. Two hours later, with my shopping stowed, I loaded my work email account on my laptop and saw the monthly circular issued to all departments that detailed current internal vacancies. One caught my eye as I scrolled down — a position in the Fiscal Policy Unit of HM Treasury that fit my experience and qualifications, not just one but two pay-grades up. I looked at the starting salary then the time-served increments to follow, thought *wow* and downloaded the application form. It took me the rest of the morning to complete the answers required before I took a deep breath and submitted it. Then I changed into my footie kit and headed out to the match.

I grinned at Lucy's slightly too-pale face as I walked into the changing room and put my sport bag on the bench. "You don't look as hungover as I thought you would."

She unzipped her trackie top and hung it on a peg. "No, Jay fed me a couple of ibuprofen after I puked then gave me a liter bottle of water to take with me to bed. Sorry if my being a total pisshead put paid to your plans."

I took my goalie gloves out of my sport bag. "No biggie. We'll catch up with each other later or whenever."

Four more of the team walked through the door, including Sarah. "The opposition's minibus has just pulled up," she said and put her holdall beside mine. "I saw that tall, red-haired center-back of theirs on board. Watch for her elbow coming your way when she jumps to head the ball in a set-piece, Ellie. She's a dirty cow!"

I nodded. "Luckily, she takes quite an obvious look around to check where the ref is when she's thinking of making the foul."

I swapped my trainers for boots, fastened my padded gloves then followed Lucy out of the door to warm up on the pitch. We jogged twice around its perimeter before the rest of the team caught up with us, then Lucy called the lunges, star jumps and stretches of our pre-match routine. I jogged to the goal and saw Liam, my mate from university who played for the men's team, warming up, ready to run the line. Woolton Wanderers, our opposition, trotted out and began their own stretching routine.

Our team lined up in front of me and took some practice shots until the referee blew his whistle to call us to order and flip the coin. Lucy won the toss, kicked off from the center spot and by half-time the score was still nil-nil and I had avoided two 'accidental' movements of the redhead's elbow toward my midriff. In the second half, her elbow came for me again, narrowly avoiding my teeth, and I brought up my knee and just as accidentally jabbed her coccyx. She fell to the ground and rolled around. The ref waved play on. I offered her my hand to stand and took my chance to growl into her ear as she accepted, "The next time you try that one, lady, you're toast."

She gave me the middle finger and stalked off but didn't come that close to me again, and we won the match one-nil. I showered, changed into my trackie then walked to the clubhouse and saw Cheryl and Sarah standing at the bar. I joined them and smirked. "Cosmopolitans all around then, is it, girls?"

Sarah made a barfing sound, while Cheryl pretended to gag then said, "Nah! Half a lager apiece."

"With lemonade to top it up," Sarah added.

I laughed and ordered two half-pints of shandy and a gin and tonic for myself. Lucy walked up to the bar, looked at our drinks and muttered, "Ew!"

I offered her my glass. "Hair of the dog. Get a mouthful down your neck?"

She took my glass and swallowed. "Okay... Yeah... I could go one of those."

I ordered her one as Liam arrived at my side and grinned. "Ellie, I didn't flag for it, but your knee was a little high."

I smiled and shrugged. "As were her elbows that could have landed me with quite a dental bill."

Liam gave me a one-armed hug around my middle. "I know. That's why I didn't call it."

Mandy, his girlfriend, called from farther down the bar, "Liam, have you seen this on Insta? Come and look..."

I puckered him an air-kiss and received a sharp look from her as he winked at me then moved to join her. Platters of hot-roasted potatoes interlaced with slices of roast beef, cooked pink to rare, appeared on the bar. We tucked in with only napkins for plates and bowls of mustard and horseradish cream to dip into. Jay walked up to the bar and sniffed. "That smells good."

I turned, leaned forward and kissed his face then giggled when he kissed me back and rubbed his face fur on my cheek. "Bear, your whiskers are super tickly today."

He moved closer to murmur, "Anywhere else you'd like to be tickled by them later?"

I smiled at the thought. "Yeah. Okay then."

Jay ordered another round of drinks while we ate and I got the next one, then we said our goodnights around the clubhouse and walked to my flat. I opened my front door and Jay followed me in. "You're in luck, Bear. I shopped this morning if you want to knock the tops off a couple of beers."

He smiled, slipped off his shoes, hung his jacket on the coat rack, walked to the fridge then handed me an open bottle. I dropped my bag beside the sofa and sat.

Jay joined me, his drink in one hand, his other arm resting along the sofa behind me. I put my bottle on the coffee table, straddled his thighs, unbuttoned his shirt and rubbed my cheek against his chest hair.

"Mmmm... cuddly."

Jay smiled and put his arm around my back. "Cuddle away."

I took his bottle from him, stood it beside mine and peeled off my tee. His chest hair tickled my breasts as I leaned close for his kiss and he pushed my breasts to his face when our lips parted and rubbed his beard against them to my giggle.

"Bear!"

He grasped my breasts, one in each hand, and flicked his tongue over my nipples. "You have the most fantastic tits, Ellie."

I pressed closer. "Suck, Bear..."

He tightened his grip and licked each hard nub then increased the suction of his mouth, and my groin responded. I traced my fingers over the erection straining against the fabric of his jeans, unfastened them, set it free from his boxers and grasped his shaft.

He released my breast and murmured. "Please, Ellie?"

I slipped off his lap, knelt between his legs, fastened my mouth over his cockhead then tugged his jeans and underwear down. He wriggled to help me. I eased them over his feet, threw them to one side and moved my mouth to his balls while sliding my hand back and forth over his shaft. His thigh hair tickled my cheeks as I licked. I raised my head, put his cock in the valley of my breasts and pressed them into his pubic bush. The rise and fall of his chest quickened. "Ellie... Yes."

My pussy wettened at his reaction. I stood, stripped off the remainder of my clothes and Jay gazed at me. I dipped my hand into my bag, took out a condom and ripped it open. "I'm going to fuck you now, Bear."

A vein throbbed down the length of his cock. "Please..."

I pinched the top of the condom and rolled it down Jay's erection to his soft whimpers, then straddled his lap, teased the tip of his shaft through my wetness and sank onto the length of him. He groaned and grasped my butt. I bounced, tilted my hips for his cock to rub on my sweet spot and muscles tightened in my groin. I ground down, rotating my pussy around his hardness until he groaned his climax while I sighed at the quietness of my orgasm that, although achieving its end goal, hadn't left me yelling, *'Oh, fuck! Yes!'*

I stilled, eased myself off his cock and he smiled as he removed the condom. "That was beautiful, Ellie. I'll use the bathroom."

I re-dressed while he was gone then turned the television on and flicked the channel to the one showing *Match of the Day.* Jay handed me my bottle, picked up his and I watched my team's match kick off.

"How come you support the London Blues when you're a Northern girl?" he asked.

"Because they were the first team I saw play live. I wasn't much into sport until uni. Chelsea are Liam's team. He took me to a match and I loved it."

"And boxing?"

I chugged a mouthful of beer, pulled my legs up and crossed them. "Yep...and golf. It's all down to Liam that I tried them and enjoyed them."

"You two...um...seem very close?"

I looked at Jay's face and laughed. "Don't you start. Mandy giving me the evil eye is enough already. Liam and I are mates. We have been for years. End of."

"Sorry," he said and rested his arm along the back of the sofa behind me. Fabregas' movement on screen caught my eye. I started to jiggle up and down as he passed a perfect ball direct to Pedro's feet, bounced faster when Pedro slotted it through to Hazard and yelled when Hazard buried the ball in the left-hand corner of the net.

"Ellie!" Jay laughed. "You'll have your neighbors complaining about the noise."

"Nah." I smiled. "They can cope with an occasional whoop from me. It's not as if I throw bass-thumping all-nighters in a flat that could hold six extra at most, standing room only."

"This is a good first buy, though—a new-build in a prime location."

I thought about the job I'd applied for. "I'd like to trade up next year. Get a place with a second bedroom so my mum and dad can stay with me when they come to Town instead of having to pay for a hotel room."

"That sounds pricey. Will your parents help you out?"

I glanced away from the telly and shook my head. "No. They're comfortable but not well off, and I wouldn't want them to, even if that was any different. I like that I've gotten this far under my own steam."

"You've done well, then. Neither Lucy nor I would have our places if our parents hadn't downsized and contributed to our mortgage deposit funds."

"As a loan?"

"Nah." He smiled. "They wanted somewhere smaller and easier to maintain for their retirement and Dad's theory was we might as well have it now as later and avoid what inheritance tax we can. We're four into the seven-year rule, so, barring an unexpected catastrophe, we'll escape the taxman's grab on the gift."

I toasted him with my bottle. "Good planning."

The crowd roared. I fixed my eyes back on the screen until the full-time whistle blew and whooped as the match ended two-nil to the Blues. An advert for the next program to be shown came on — *A Place In The Sun* — France. Jay watched the teaser snippets being shown and asked, "What would you reckon, Ellie, to us having a week away together in Paris?"

I hesitated. I liked Jay, but to be in his company twenty-four-seven gave me pause, so I skirted his suggestion. "I'll have to take a pass on that. I applied for a new job this morning and need to stay flexible, without any firm plans for the next few months."

He sat a little straighter. "Just because of that or because you want to stay flexible all around?"

I swallowed a mouthful of my beer. "Erm... That's the basis we're seeing each other on, Jay."

"I was hoping we could see more of each other? Be more of a couple?"

I looked into his eyes and the thought of not seeing Mark again if I committed to a steady relationship gave me my answer. I shook my head. "I'm sorry. I'm not ready for that."

He returned my gaze. "It's not Liam, but there's someone else in the picture, isn't there? In the background...just out of sight."

I nodded. "Yeah, someone I see now and then that I can't promise to steer clear of from here on in. I'd be lying if I did."

Jay brushed his fingertips down the side of my face. "I suspected as much and I'm sorry too, then, Ellie. If that's the way things are for you, I need to get out before I'm in over my head."

I captured his hand and held it to my cheek. "I'd hate for you to be hurt by me, Bear. There are reasons why things stand the way they do with me, so yeah, for the best, you should."

Jay stood, leaned down and kissed my cheek. "I can't say it doesn't hurt, but you never promised me anything more. I know that. I'll tell Lucy we've decided to move on from one another. No drunken angst and no awkward moments if we meet in the future."

I looked into his beautiful brown eyes. "Take care, Jay. I'm truly sorry I can't be what you need."

He smiled a small smile, put his jacket and shoes on then let himself out of the front door. I picked up our bottles, put them in the trash and went to bed wishing I could feel sadder over our break-up instead of a mild sense of relief that it had ended without too much collateral damage to a lovely but not-the-one-for-me man.

* * * *

Four days later, an email from Mark dropped into my inbox, and behind the privacy of my closed office door, I smiled as I read the name of the top-ranked audit company he'd chosen then smiled wider as I opened the email below it to read that my application for the position in the Treasury Department had resulted in an invitation for me to attend for an interview.

I looked at their email again, noted the upgrade in security vetting required for the role and realized that the close scrutiny I would receive during the application process meant I must stay away from Mark until the job was either mine or not. I wrinkled my nose at the thought but stiffened my resolve for the financial security that would be mine if I landed the role, along with the groin-tingling prospect that I would also be free of the regulatory personal interests register and able to see Mark upfront and in public if he wanted.

Two weeks later, I attended my first interview and three weeks after that, a second one, before a board of its five most high and mighty. Mark's external audit results arrived the same week and, not without protests of longing from between my legs, I emailed him a request to clarify a couple of points rather than extend the invitation 'to attend these offices and discuss' I would normally have sent.

My formal offer of the Treasury role arrived not long after, in the same week as the Christmas lights were strung up in Oxford Street to be turned on by the current trending celebrity in the retail trade's annual attempt to convince the buying public that the festive season began in early November. I opened the email, reviewed the terms and conditions attached, noted the January start date then logged onto my work admin account and booked annual leave to use my accrued holiday allowance. Next, I scrolled down the options and lit up the box marked 'Resign' then clicked on the reason—'Internal Transfer'. My walk up the stairs to make a courtesy call to the 'Chief Regulator on High' completed the process and I Skyped my mum with the news when I got home.

I released my hair and took off my specs as my laptop loaded on the coffee table. My mum's face appeared on screen as our webcams connected with the familiar outline of our country kitchen behind her.

"Ellie, love. A call on a Thursday? What's up?"

I looked at the question in her hazel eyes, her face surrounded by waves of soft chestnut hair that fell just past her shoulders like mine, and smiled.

"Nothing's up. I got an email today. I applied for promotion and got it."

Mum beamed. "Oh, love, that's wonderful. The same department or — ?"

"No. A move to the Fiscal Policy Unit at the Treasury and two pay-grades up. I finish at the Regulatory Office at Christmas and start in my new position after the New Year holiday."

"Wow, Ellie. A double promotion. Well done."

"Thanks, Mum. I'll be home a few days earlier than usual for Christmas. I've got some annual leave owing to take."

"Ah…" she said. "Yes, Christmas…"

I looked at the small crease lines that appeared at the side of her eyes as she hesitated. "What about Christmas, Mum?"

"Um…" she said, wrinkling her nose. "He might not have been back to the village since Sebastian…but I saw Lorraine in the post office yesterday and she said Tim is coming home for the holiday."

My stomach clenched as she said the name, but I kept my reply breezy against the tension of her shoulders and the bead of worry in her eyes. "Well, I daresay I'll be able to keep a civil tongue in my head if I have to speak to him after all these years."

Her shoulders relaxed. "I'm sure we can avoid him most of the time, apart from Louisa's party, although I can excuse us from going for a tummy bug or something, if you like."

I curled my hands into fists out of sight of the webcam but managed to keep my voice even. "No. It wasn't me that behaved like a shit. It was him. I'll try to avoid him where I can but I'm not going into hiding because he's back in the village. We'll go to Louisa's party like we always do."

"That's the way, love." Mum smiled. "Chin up and ignore him. I'll tell Dad your good news. He'll be thrilled."

"Thanks, Mum. Tell him I'll Skype after the match on Saturday. Bye. Speak soon."

I cut my cam connection to Mum's wave of goodbye, closed my laptop then went to my bedroom and changed into a trackie and training shoes. Two hours later I let myself back into my flat, feeling better for an hour wearing boxing gloves and pummeling the life out of the punching bag at the gym, then showered and rustled up a cheese omelet. My phone rang as I turned on the television and sat on the sofa. I put my earbuds in when I saw it was Liam calling and I carried on talking hands-free while I ate.

"Ellie, I know it's short notice but I'm desperate for a favor on Saturday night if you're not busy?" he said.

"I was going to have a drink or several with the girls in the clubhouse after the match but I can give it a miss if it's important. Shoot. What's up?"

"A swankfest of a charity do I can't get out of for work. I need a plus one. Mandy has come down with a stinking cold and can't go with me. I'm going to look like a right sad idiot if I have an empty seat beside me at the table."

I hesitated. Liam and I had been 'special' friends for a while in our early days at uni, and Mandy's occasional sharp glances in my direction told me she didn't quite believe we'd moved past the sex but still liked each other enough to stay good mates.

"She's okay with me standing in, is she?"

"Sorry, Ellie, but it's her problem if she's not. I've been nothing but honest with her or I wouldn't have told her about us in the first place. You and I have a bit of history from our fresher's year but that was ten years ago. Mandy can believe me or not. It's her choice."

I heard the undertone of hurt in his voice and guessed at his need for a make or break, line-in-the-sand scenario. "Okay. Sure. I'm up for it. What time and where?"

Liam blew a kiss down the line. "Thanks, Ellie. Black tie in the Savoy ballroom but a taxi is included in my allowable expenses, so I'll pick you up at yours around six-thirty."

I blew a kiss back, cut the call then dumped my plate in the sink and walked upstairs just before midnight. My call to Mum came back to me as I got into bed. I pushed away the memories it stirred as I closed my eyes, but my unconscious mind still drifted to the summer after I'd turned seventeen…

Tim arrived home from uni as I studied for my last exam to be taken the following week. We met every day, kissed, laughed and exchanged silly promises of love forever, and I willingly handed him my virginity in a moment of unprotected stupidity one red-hot scorching afternoon that resulted in the birth of our child, far too early, not quite six months later.

Tim held my hand and I stroked Sebastian's tiny face with the fingertips of my other while we watched the rise and fall of his chest as he lay in the incubator, and we held each other tight when his body gave up the fight for life after four days. I returned home, numb and empty until the following week, when the birth and death certificates for Sebastian Timothy McAllister fell through the letterbox in the same envelope, then cried as if I would never stop.

Mum made the necessary calls to the mortuary and the undertaker and arranged Sebastian's service of blessing and cremation. A week later I stood outside the chapel and waited for Tim, then sat inside it without him and watched the small, white, satin-covered casket containing our son carried down the aisle in the arms of the undertaker. My solitary tears ran down my face throughout the service and committal, and my bewildered voicemails, texts and emails to Tim remained unanswered in the days that followed until I gave up trying...

I woke in the morning, heavy-eyed, took a hot shower and locked the memories away in the only way I knew how, by focusing on work, work and only work until my mind was so full of it that nothing else remained. For the rest of the day I protected myself against their return with a mixture of fierce concentration while at the office and plenty of evening time in the gym to ensure I slept the deeper sleep of the well-worn-out that night.

* * * *

Saturday morning dawned with the kind of deluge that would churn a football pitch to mud if it were played on. I checked my phone, saw the match had been canceled, so texted Dad the news, threw my contraceptive pill down my throat then snuggled back beneath my duvet and didn't surface again until after midday. A plate of scrambled eggs and bacon later, I surveyed my legs and quim then toddled off to the wet-room to de-fuzz them.

After I toweled dry, I put on my bathrobe and opened my not over-full wardrobe that had my work suits hanging to the left and, on the right, just enough evening wear to satisfy my liking to don the glad-rags when offered the chance to do so. For a black-tie event, my full-length dresses amounted to a choice of two—

one turquoise that fit to the hip then finished in layers of floating chiffon or one midnight blue with shoestring straps that hugged every inch of me from bust to floor. The rain still pounding on the windows decided for me. Chiffon belonged to balmy summer evenings, the stretch-velvet of darker blue to November rain.

I laid my choice on my bed, stepped into a seam-free invisible thong and fastened a strapless bra that flattered my breasts rather than squashing them. I then spent the next two hours giving my face the full works with shading, plenty of eyeliner, false lashes and full red, red lips. Next, I faced the trickier task of lengthening my fingernails that I kept short to suit the sports I played, glanced at my dress and acknowledged my hands would be next to useless once I'd glued the extensions on. I looked at the time on my phone, saw it was nearly five so walked downstairs, flicked the telly from Sky Sport to a chart music channel and uncapped a bottle of beer while I still had hands that worked properly.

My bottle in hand, I walked upstairs, shimmied into my dress and captured the sides of my hair with a diamante clip behind each ear that allowed it to rest on my shoulders in thickened waves. I spent the rest of the hour attaching fiddly false nails and painting them to match the color of my lipstick. I blew on them until the varnish was set then swapped cards and cash from my work purse into my evening clutch and added my phone and door key. My phone trilled with a message of 'Outside' from Liam at six-twenty, so I stepped up onto six-inch spiked heels, donned my knee-length, hooded parka against the rain and went to meet him.

The taxi waited at the curb with its passenger door open. I leapt inside. Liam reached across and slammed it shut as I pushed my hood back from my hair. "God,

Liam! You couldn't have picked a worse night. Will it keep many people away?"

Liam grinned. He was tall and rangy, with a mop of dark curls on his head, an infectious smile and sparkling eyes. "I wouldn't think so, being as the bash is in aid of the permanently soggy RNLI."

I smiled then laughed as it occurred to me. "Ah... Excuse me for being thick, but why is the homeless charity you work for supporting the national lifeboat rescue service?"

"It's not." He winked. "However, Mrs. Judy Sneed, the Right Honorable Member of Parliament who also happens to be on the Charity Commission Board, is the guest speaker tonight. We've booked tickets, two at a time, to fill any spare places at the tables in the hope that one of us will able to bend her ear at some point during the evening."

I snorted. "Liam, that's outrageous!"

"I know." He laughed. "But it's dog-eat-dog in the charity world. There's only so much goodwill to go around."

The cab pulled up at the Savoy and the liveried doorman opened the car door holding a large umbrella to escort us to the entrance. Liam palmed him a twenty-pound note as he showed us in. He muttered into my ear, "On expenses to add to the general goodwill."

We walked into the foyer and I handed my parka to the cloakroom assistant. Liam offered me his arm. "Thanks, Ellie. You look beautiful and I appreciate it."

I raised my nose in the air and sniffed. "Don't I always?"

"No," he smiled. "I can't say the sight of you in the mud or sweat of your more normal sportswear is that."

I side-swiped his arm. "That's the trouble with you. Fussy, fussy, fussy!"

Liam grinned and we sauntered through to the pre-dinner reception room, picked up a glass of fizz apiece from the offered tray then walked over to the ballroom door to look at the table plan posted outside it. He ran his finger over the names. "Good. We're spread around the room. Jim and Claire are closest to the Minister on the Sundowner table, number two. We're with Tooting Incorporated on eight. Elaine and Luke are with Walker and Timpson, table five."

I looked at the positioning of the tables on the plan, saw Mark's name then that of his partner, Ms. Angel Devine, thought *Shit!* and wrinkled my nose. "That last lot are part of my caseload at work. I'd prefer not to spend my evening in their direct eyeline. Let's sneak in and swap the place cards around so all they get to see of us is our backs."

"Sure thing," Liam agreed and removed his jacket. "Stay here. I'll slip in. Without my jacket, I'll just be taken for a waiter doing a table check if anyone is looking."

I held his jacket and he returned a couple of minutes later. "Done."

I smiled my relief at not having to eat my dinner with Mark, alongside his girlfriend, date or other occasional bedmate, in view and handed Liam his jacket while silently chastising myself for not discovering that the theme of the event was one that could well be supported by a man who loved watersports before I accepted the invite. We moved away from the ballroom door with our drinks and I used my six-foot-plus high-heeled height to scan the reception room for any sight of Mark's dark-blond hair while resting lightly on the balls of my feet to turn my back to him should I do so, until the master of ceremonies called us to order and we made our way to our table.

Liam pulled out my chair for me. I sat and studied the menu card as the room filled and the volume of chatter rose to blend all conversation into a generally indistinct buzz. Our table introduced itself as wine was poured and Liam went to work, charming and urbane as he spoke, while I sat beside him to nod, smile, add the odd comment where needed and provide his eye-candy. The meal moved through its courses until a comfort break was announced while coffee and liqueurs were ordered and served.

Three of our table excused themselves, while more guests did the same as serving staff moved forward to clear the detritus of napkins, menu cards and place markers. Liam turned around on his chair and looked at the top table, ready to move and take a seat on it if the chance presented itself. He smiled and nudged my arm. "Mission accomplished. I swear Jim's as fast as a striking snake. His butt was planted on the chair beside her seconds after the bloke who was sat on it stood and excused himself."

"Good work, that man," I said.

Liam looked at his watch. "We don't have to stay for the after-dinner waffle now if you'd like to give it a miss."

"Thank the Lord for that." I smiled. "Give me ten to visit the Ladies and we'll leg it."

"Sure. Grab your coat when you're done and call me from the foyer. I'll offer our excuses to the table and come on out."

I nodded, stood and kept my eyes fixed firmly on nowhere but the exit as I made my way through the room. The sign for the Ladies caught my eye as I walked out, in a corner to the left of the cloakroom, so I claimed my coat on my way to it and found the early rush to the loo had been and gone when I pushed open the door. I used the cubicle, washed my hands and decided to lurk outside beneath the hotel's canopy in my anonymously shapeless parka while I waited for Liam. I pulled open the door, walked out and heard Mark's voice to the side of me.

"Ellie?"

My heart double tapped. I turned, saw him leaning against the wall and ignored the tummy flutters urging me to walk closer and touch. "Loitering, Mr. Walker? Outside of the ladies' toilets. Really?"

He straightened then stepped closer until I could smell the Armani cologne he always wore. I gazed into the predatory gleam that lit his eyes when he was turned on as he murmured, "You look stunning, Ellie."

His very kissable lips only inches from mine, I took in a deeper breath. "A very risky venture into my personal space, Mr. Walker. We are in public view."

He locked his eyes on mine. "What's there to see? It's just two people talking. That's all."

My nipples hardened in response to his closeness and my mouth watered, although my lips felt dry. I moistened them with the tip of my tongue. "I don't think talking is uppermost in your mind any more than it is in mine."

"No. It's not. So?"

Muscles tightened in my groin until my business brain kicked into gear to remind me the hotel was full of CCTV cameras and I was still vulnerable to the withdrawal of my Treasury job offer should any indiscretion of mine come to light before the day I walked out of the Regulatory Office for the last time. I broke our eye contact and stepped back. "So, I'm exiting stage left before anyone comes across us looking at each other like we haven't just eaten dinner. Goodnight, Mr. Walker."

His lips tilted to a half-smile. "Night then, my lovely she-dragon. I'll wait to hear from you through work."

I shrugged into my parka, took my phone out of my bag and called Liam as I walked to the vestibule. He joined me a few minutes later and the doorman beckoned forward a taxi. We climbed inside. Liam gave the driver my address then called Mandy. I listened to his one-sided conversation.

"Yes, I'm on my way home. Yes, before ten. I told you it was a work function, not a night on the town. My mate dug me out of a hole and came with me. That's all."

He winked at me. "No, Ellie's gone home. I got the taxi to drop her off at her flat." Then he grinned. "Yes, I'll stop off at the shop to buy you a packet of cold and flu Lemsip and come tuck you into bed."

The taxi drew up outside my apartment block as he cut the call and I laughed as I stepped out of it. "Enjoy the rest of your night. I'll see you at footie training on Wednesday."

"Night and thanks," he said as I shut the cab door.

I peeled off my false nails and lashes after I closed my front door, changed into PJs then put *Match of the Day* on the television and sat on the sofa with a packet of makeup wipes. I colored the moist tissue as I watched but found the game not holding my attention after bumping into Mark. I glanced at the time and wondered what he would have done if I'd replied, 'So, take me to bed' rather than stepping away, then whether he was now in bed with his date instead of me. I huffed and dropped the wipe into the bin then huffed some more at the silent debate taking place inside my head.

I don't know why you're huffing. It was you that set the rules. You meet up every so often and in between times you date other guys and he dates other girls.

Yes. Okay. But why the hell did I have to find out her name?

What difference does it make?

I hate it when a bedmate I'm sharing a guy's time with becomes a 'somebody' rather than a vague 'could be anyone at all'.

Well, it could be worse. At least you still don't know what she looks like.

As both sides of my argument agreed whole-heartedly with that statement, I turned the television off and went to bed.

Chapter Three

I woke on Sunday and saw the men's match had been postponed, like ours, so with no live footie to support, I headed to the gym and spent several hours sparring and punching the bag to make sure my unconscious brain wandered nowhere while I slept. On Monday, the rain finally ceased, and I walked into my office ahead of time, ready for the week ahead.

I loaded my email account as I sat behind my desk and clicked open the one that had 'Re: Your Replacement' in the subject line. I read that Evelynn Price had been promoted to the position of regulator from her current role as a legal exec, with immediate effect. I looked at the work table that ran at a right angle to the side of my desk and re-filed the spillover of folders onto the floor then captured a spare office chair and added it. Evelynn appeared at my office door promptly at nine and I motioned toward the work table.

"Congratulations. Come on in and take a pew."

She put her attaché case beside the chair, sat and looked at the bare table top. "What have you done with it all?"

I nodded over my shoulder. "I've filed it on the floor."

She looked at the color-coded rainbow behind me. "I've left the same behind in Legal — yougov.com's not really on board with paperless data entry yet, is it?"

"Of course it is," I said, "so long as every paperless entry is backed up by hard copy in triplicate, just in case."

She raised an eyebrow and gave me a whimsical shrug. "Lead on then, McDuff, and show me my fate."

I let a small what-the-hell, I'm-outta-here-soon smile cross my face and handed her three folders to read while I continued cross-referencing Mark's audit report, and two weeks flew past, with Evelynn so familiar with the role as to need only a little background history and some guidance on technique from me while I worked on the Walker and Timpson proposal with the aim of authorizing it — or not — before I left.

During the third week, I made my decision to authorize, having caught not so much as a whiff of a potential subsidiary company in the UK or offshore, nor found any monies sitting in any account where they shouldn't be. I emailed my decision to Legal then spent the fourth week walking Evelynn through the proposed scheme.

"And I'll have to authorize this?" she asked on Friday.

I shook my head. "No. I've sent my decision through to Legal for the letter of authorization to be prepared, so it won't fall to you."

"Then my blessings to you, my sweet." She smiled. "I'm more than happy to monitor the outcome but even happier it will not be my signature on the dotted line that legalized this. When will you sign and inform them?"

Four weeks of Evelynn's blunt replies and the humor that accompanied them, alongside my touch of end-of-term fever, relaxed my face into a smile. "I've authorized it, but as it will be your head on the block from here on in, I'll let them have my decision when you tell me you're comfortable with the scheme."

She caught my eye with hers and poised her finger over Mark's business address. "Offices in Brighton. The Lanes. The Churchill Centre. What are the chances of an overnighter to fit in a little necessary Christmas shopping while we're about our business?"

My tummy fluttered at her words. "When were you thinking of?"

Evelynn scrolled through her phone. "How about some time during the week of the thirteenth to the seventeenth? *The Rocky Horror Show* is on at the Brighton Centre and I wouldn't mind catching that."

My heart thumped as she suggested a date so irresistibly close to the finishing line that I nodded. "I believe I have enough left in my expenses budget for a final overnight trip, and a formal handover would be warranted for this, I should say. I'll make it my swan song. I have some holiday days accrued that I'm taking, so if we go to Brighton on the sixteenth, I'll announce our decision in person and introduce you as my replacement on my last working day, the seventeenth."

"Perfect." She smiled. "I'll whizz a group text out to my mates to see who's up for the show then look at the available tickets online."

I left her to tap on her phone while I emailed Mark my request for a meeting at his offices and received my first-ever less-than-professional reply from him five minutes later.

Ms. McAllister,
With so many weeks gone by without personal contact 'with' you, please accept my thanks for your 'finally' managing to fit me into your busy schedule. I will see you on the date suggested if your risk assessment of venturing to Brighton proves to be satisfactory.
Mark

I smiled at the twist he'd put on my words from the night at the Savoy and replied with a little mis-wording of my own.

Mr. Walker,
Thank you for your patience. It is indeed sometimes difficult to 'wrestle' a little time out of my schedule. My risk assessment suggested the advisability of inviting you to attend our offices was inappropriate due to the sensitive nature of a project being undertaken by myself. That now complete, I am happy to attend 'to you', in person, on the date suggested.
E.M.

I pressed Send and snorted as I read his near instant riposte.

Ms. McAllister,
I look forward to receiving your personal attention in the matter and will do my best to satisfy your requirements also.
Mark

I grinned at my screen and Evelynn looked at me. "Something funny tickling you?"

I straightened my face. "Just a couple of typos on an email."

Mark made several appearances in my head during the rest of the day, most of the time naked. I kept goal the next afternoon and let two past me through lack of concentration then faced my opponent in the ring that evening in far too happy a frame of mind until she glanced a shot across my jaw that hurt. I launched my right hand toward her cheekbone, swiftly followed by a solid left hook to her chin that rocked her from her feet and planted her butt firmly on the canvas to the referee's count of ten.

I spat out my mouth guard as I danced to my corner and received Liam's wet sponge straight into my face while I spluttered. "Bastard! Pack it in!" He laughed and dropped the sponge into the bucket while I looked over his shoulder at Mandy, sitting ringside, mimed a drinking action and mouthed the word 'Curry'. Mandy, at ease in my company since the night Liam had left the charity dinner early, smiled and gave me a thumb's-up. I showered, changed into jeans, trainers and a clean sweat top then met them at the door of the small, unprofitable cinema now turned boxing venue.

Mandy threaded her arm through Liam's and we walked toward the smell of savory meat and spices, entering a restaurant wreathed in scents to make my stomach rumble. A melted cheese and garlic naan bread later, I pushed my plate of unfinished prawn dopiaza away and undid the top button of my jeans. "Bugger. I've got no more room."

Liam lifted his butt cheek as if he was letting out a little gas. "There's always a way to make a little more room."

I glanced at Mandy and nudged her arm. "When we knew each other a little better than we do now, he used to trap my head under the bedcovers when he did that for real. And he wouldn't even let me out when I gagged."

She snorted. "Liam! You are a disgusting sod!"

I laughed. "I hope he's outgrown it! The stinky git!"

Mandy laughed with me. "He has, although I won't venture anywhere near the loo for at least fifteen minutes after he's been enthroned."

"Too much information, ladies." Liam smirked and Mandy and I hooted.

Liam called a taxi as the waiter cleared our table. They dropped me home and took the cab on while I climbed into bed and fell asleep to thoughts of the taste of Mark's mouth and the feel of his muscled body pressed against mine.

* * * *

Sunday passed in a whirl of football. I watched the men's team draw their match then joined my own teammates in the clubhouse for a low-voiced pow-wow over a few drinks to discuss our tactics for the upcoming girls versus guys charity match to be played between Christmas Day and New Year's. At work on Monday, I began to clear any outstanding issues from my non-Walker and Timpson caseload and, by Friday, found I had so little work left to complete that I called up the Walker and Timpson website, clicked on the picture of 'Our CEO' and indulged my pussy tingles by designing a spreadsheet macro to count down the days and hours remaining until I saw him.

Over the weekend, I ordered the cakes and iced buns that anyone leaving the department not under a cloud was expected to supply, along with flowers and chocolates to be delivered to Joanne and Leza. I opened the patisserie boxes and laid them on the table beside the coffee machine on Wednesday and received my signed-by-everybody card, along with my time-served crystal decanter from our beloved leader, during the afternoon. The next day, I sat opposite Evelynn on the train to Brighton, my pussy damp with anticipation as I counted down the final hours. My heart sped up as the train pulled into the station and tummy-tickling butterflies joined it as Evelynn and I made our way to the town center and shopped to the sound of live music from buskers and bars as we walked up and down The Lanes.

The afternoon rolled on until darkness fell and the sparkle of Christmas lights joined the street lamps. Evelynn puffed out and pointed toward a bar a little farther up the street. I smiled my agreement and plonked my bags alongside hers as we sat at a table inside to the sound of a jazz band doing extraordinary things to the normal melodies of various Christmas carols.

Evelynn looked at the time on her phone. "Good. It's not quite five. I've plenty of time to eat then get ready for the show."

I nodded, and with my body alive with a need that didn't include food, ordered a small plate of salad and a large glass of cold white wine. Evelynn selected a chargrilled steak to be accompanied by an equally large glass of red, and when our order arrived, I drank more than I ate then settled the bill before we walked to our hotel. Evelynn went ahead of me to prepare for her show after we'd registered while I stayed at reception to request a second card key, which I left behind the desk in an envelope with my room number and Mark's name written on it.

I opened the door after a short ride in the lift and found the room identical to every other room I'd occupied in the hotel over the last couple of years. I dumped my shopping bags on the wardrobe floor and opened my overnight bag. My silk, thigh-length wrap sat on top, and I took it with my toiletry bag to the bathroom and showered, my skin flushing in anticipation of Mark's touch as I soaped up. Toweled dry, I slipped on my wrap then hung my suit in the wardrobe, placed a square of additional prevention under the pillow and dried my hair.

The door clicked open as I replaced the hairdryer in the dressing table drawer. Mark walked in not wearing his tie, his shirt collar loosened and his suit jacket over his arm. Shivers raced down my spine as I stood to meet him and I saw a hunger in his eyes to match mine.

He dropped his jacket onto the chair and pulled me into his arms. "Jesus, Ellie! You've never made me wait this long..."

I wrapped my arms around his neck, lifted my face for his kiss and *her* name popped into my head. "I don't imagine you've gone short."

His cock hardened against my thigh. "We play by *your* rules, Ellie, not mine."

I put an end to a subject I hadn't meant to raise with a kiss. Mark tugged on the belt of my robe and I plucked at the buttons of his shirt. He deepened our kiss, his mouth hot and urgent as he pushed my wrap over my shoulders.

I stepped backward to the bed as it fell to the floor, lay on it then cupped and squeezed my breasts. "Come and play, then."

His irises darkened as he took off his shirt. My heart rate increased as I looked at his chest and the ripped muscles of his belly. I stroked my pussy as I watched him unfasten his zip and ease his trousers and boxers down and off—his cock erect, the head of it glistening. I offered him my fingers, wet with my juices. He lay beside me, licked the taste of me from them, grasped my breast and fastened his mouth over my nipple. I threaded my fingers through the back of his hair and arched my back to meet his greedy suck. He tugged and extended my nipple with his teeth to my writhe of pleasure then kneaded and worked his magic until I gasped, "Mark…"

He lifted his head and nibbled my bottom lip. "I need to taste more of you."

"And me you…" I breathed.

I whimpered as he kissed down my body then twisted and moved his legs so I could reach his cock. I caressed his shaft as he explored the creases of my pussy, then I took him into my mouth and sucked in rhythm to the movement of my hand. He stroked between my pussy lips and my breathing accelerated as he brushed his warm tongue over my swollen clit. I moved my mouth, sought out the sweet spot behind his already-full balls and they tightened as I probed, the rise and fall of his chest quickening against my thigh. I grasped the base of his shaft, squeezed and increased the pressure of my tongue. He groaned as his balls swelled a little more. "God, Ellie. Please now…"

I released his cock, felt under the pillow for the condom, ripped it open and rolled it down his length. He righted himself. I opened my legs and he stroked through my wetness then plunged his shaft inside me. I lifted my hips to meet him, panting. He moaned and thrust deeper and faster. I sucked on his shoulder as the throb of my clit built, and I wrapped my legs around his thighs, digging my fingers into his back.

He stiffened, his breath hot in my ear. "Slap. Do it."

I slapped his butt cheek. He tensed. "Yes…"

I smacked harder, then on his other side, and he groaned his orgasm. I ground against him, my pussy pulsating with the waves of my climax while I mewled with pleasure. We stilled, breathing hard, and I caressed the contours of his back as our heart rates steadied. He kissed my lips then my neck, eased his cock out and removed the condom. I relaxed against him and adjusted the squash of my breasts on his chest to his murmur of appreciation.

"Mmmm… I've missed you, my little she-dragon."

I put my leg across his thigh and cuddled in tighter. "Yeah? And me you."

He kissed into my hair. "What kept you away? Are you okay?"

I nuzzled into his chest. "My security vetting was up for review, so I had to steer clear. Any whiff of us being together like this would have meant do-not-pass-go-and-collect-two-hundred for me and down-the-slippery-snake-back-to-square-one for your current request for authorization, but I've been given the green good-to-go light again now."

Mark tightened his arm around me. "Nosy bastards! I think I saw one of your legal execs in the lobby when I arrived. I couldn't be absolutely sure with the way she was dressed, but I ducked out of the way, just in case."

"Evelynn's with me. What was she wearing?"

"Well, not a lot really. High-heels, a corset, stockings and a coat over her shoulders just about sums it up. But it was her makeup and hair that had me patting my pockets in the hope that a bulb of garlic or a crucifix might turn up in one of them."

I giggled. "That sounds about right. *The Rocky Horror Show* is on at the Brighton Centre tonight and she has tickets."

"Of course it is. I'd forgotten." He smiled. "I just hope I'll be able to look at her with a straight face tomorrow." He stroked down my back. "Ah...tomorrow? You don't normally make a client visit unless..."

I saw no need to cloak the reassurance of my decision behind vague words, with the end of my time as a regulator on the horizon, and smiled. "Our visit here is pure indulgence. I could have scanned a copy of your authorization to you and posted the original, but Evelynn and I wanted to escape the office for a bit. We've been Christmas shopping all day with more of the same to come tomorrow until we stagger into your office at four."

Mark pinched my butt. "You're telling me you've signed it?"

"Yep."

He grinned then laughed. "Did you really just say that to me ahead of the meeting? Whoa! Who's abducted my she-dragon and left this alien in her place?"

I leaned up on my elbow and kissed the end of his nose. "Well...just so I don't disappoint, I'll pop your happy balloon for you. There's still the ongoing monitoring of your compliance to come and I'm saying nada about that, because it's not going to be down to me. I've managed to get my arse kicked upstairs."

He leaned up and faced me. "You've been promoted? That's why you had to have a new security vetting?"

"Yep." I smiled. "From Vice-Principal to Deputy Director."

He sat straighter. "Oh, wow, Ellie! That deserves a bottle of fizz at least. Your legal exec must be well into her show by now. I'll go down to the bar and bring one up."

I looked at the digital display on the beside clock. "I'd love some, but hot meals finish on room service in a half-hour. I've eaten, but if you haven't, I'll order it with your dinner?"

"But I meant to treat you, not put it on your tab."

I reached up and stroked his cheek. "Then the next one's yours."

He captured my hand and kissed me with his soft, warm lips on the center of my palm then followed it with a flick from the tip of his tongue to the shiver of goosebumps down my spine. I took my hand away and traced my fingertip down his chest. "Enough on the erogenous zones before dinner, Mr. Walker."

He looked his promise into my eyes. "I shall find them after... Especially the sensitive spot in your middle that makes you squeal."

I gazed back and licked my lips. "If you win... Otherwise, I'm going to tease your cock until you beg."

"Yeah, please," he breathed.

I laughed, swung my legs off the bed and handed him the menu. "I'll get you a robe."

I picked up my wrap and walked to the bathroom, used the loo and returned with one of the hotel's toweling bathrobes, leaving the other pristinely untouched on its hanger behind the door. I handed it to him. He shrugged it on then took the condom to the bathroom while I mixed us both a drink from the mini-bar and flicked the television on for some background music. He nodded toward the menu when he returned to the bedroom. "I think a Caesar salad then the salmon fillet to go with fizz, if that's okay?"

"Sure." I smiled. "I'll order a cheese platter for the dessert course and nibble on it while you eat."

Mark puckered me an air-kiss accompanied by his flirtatious 'Newman' wink. I snorted then used the room phone to place our order as he picked up his clothes from the floor and put them in the wardrobe out of sight. I sat at the table and sipped.

He raised his glass. "Congratulations, then."

I smiled. "Thanks. I'm pretty stoked about it. I'll be able to upgrade my flat — get myself some more square footage and a second bedroom."

"Mine's got plenty of floor space and a couple of bedrooms, but that's at Brighton prices, not London. Has your place risen in value much since you bought it?" he asked.

I nodded. "A fair bit. I paid just over three hundred thousand and it should sell around the mid four hundreds now. I can go to about seven hundred next, which I'll have to if I want another purpose-built rather than a flat in a house conversion."

"Pricey, but worth it," he agreed, "for the fastest rising property values in the country."

A tap sounded on the door. Mark stood and kissed into my hair on his way past me as he took his drink into the bathroom. I straightened his chair, took a ten-pound note from my purse and opened the bedroom door. The waiter wheeled the dinner trolley in, swept his eyes over the solitary female possessions in the room then looked at me — or more particularly, as I followed the direction of his eyes, the shortness of my wrap and the shape of me beneath it. He fluttered his long, dark eyelashes as his hand hovered over the champagne bottle in the ice bucket. "If madam would like, I could serve? Or be of service?"

I stared my best 'regulatory' look at him. "I think not." Then I held out the bank note. "Shut the door quietly on your way out."

He twitched the money from my hand. "Of course, madam."

Mark opened the bathroom door after the bedroom door clicked shut and grinned. "Not again, Ellie."

I pushed fictional spectacles down my nose and looked at him. "Mr. Walker, do not try to tell me that in all the overnighters you've had in the many hotels you stayed at that you've not had the same innuendo suggested? Let alone the drool-pool that follows you around the office."

He laughed. "Drool-pool? Ew!"

I drank the last mouthful in my tall glass. "There's positive puddles of the stuff in your wake every time you walk through the place."

He picked up the champagne bottle, released the cork and poured into two clean glasses from the mini-bar. "Back at you, then. There was plenty of drool following you around the room at the Savoy from what I saw, including mine."

I smiled and steered the conversation away from talk of a night that might lead to the uncomfortable topic of other bedmates being raised — and more particularly the possibility of my learning more about Ms. Angel Devine than just her name, which was already plenty. I removed the cloche from the small plate and lifted his salad onto the table. "That looks okay tonight. Not drowned in too much dressing, anyway."

I added my cheese plate to the table, sat and picked up my glass of fizz as he sat beside me and dug into his salad. "So, are you heading for the slopes for Christmas this year or following your parents and sister to the sun?" I asked.

Mark sipped his wine and finished his salad then swapped the plate for the one containing his salmon. "No, I'm skiing again. I just can't take heat at Christmas. It's not right. I'm driving to Larry's on the twenty-second and we fly out of Manchester to the

Alpine du Maurice resort on Christmas Eve. How about you?"

I smiled and let out a small hint of what I was holding back until it was actually fait accompli the following day. "The village of Little Tinkling calls me home, as ever. I have some holiday days owing, so at close of business tomorrow, I wave bye-bye to the Regulatory Office and don't return to work until early January."

"You'll be home in plenty of time for your friend's annual party then. Are you spending all your time off with your parents?"

I nibbled on my cheese-topped cracker. "No, I've promised to keep goal at the club's fundraiser on the thirtieth. Ladies versus the men on the all-weather pitch. It was a good laugh last year and we drew quite a crowd."

"What do you do?" he smiled. "Even the odds? Tie the guys' bootlaces together or something?"

I sipped and cut another slice of cheese. "Not quite, but we do cheat, and they have to play in drag while we only have to wear Cheeky Girl shorts. Last year the theme was fairies, with an additional rule that every time one of them dropped their magic wand, the girls were awarded a penalty. The final score was twelve-nil to us."

Mark put his knife and fork on his plate and picked up his phone. "Cheeky Girl shorts, is it? Time for a little search on YouTube, I think."

I raised my eyes heavenward with a small tut as his fingers typed 'Forest Hill Charity Football Match' into the search bar, then smiled, safe in the knowledge that in the videos that had been posted of last year's match, Liam was unrecognizable and Mark watching the footage wouldn't lead to the subject of the Savoy rearing its ugly head again.

"Yep, here you are," he said then grinned as the vid showed the curve of my butt cheeks peeking beneath my shorts as I dove full-length to save a shot from Tony, dressed in a pink tutu, a matching pink beehive wig, strap-on fairy wings and a full-face of 'pantomime dame' makeup. In the background, Lucy took her chance to knock Liam's wand from his hand with her elbow and call the ref's attention to the matter, to Mark's snorted, "First class cheating there, that girl."

I laughed. "The guys are doomed again this year. The theme is American cheerleaders with pom-poms, although they might get us next year if Mandy's side-show does its job, as she keeps ribbing me it will."

"Mandy?" he asked and refilled our glasses.

I named Liam's shirt number rather than a name Mark might remember from the table plan, if he'd checked it out as I had. "The girlfriend of the opposition's number ten. She's rounded up a bunch of non-playing girlfriends and wives to dress the same as the men and perform a cheerleading routine to encourage more donations into the blue buckets rather than the pink."

"Because whichever color bucket contains the most money decides the next theme?" he guessed.

I sipped my wine and nodded. "Yeah. The guys will stay in the spirit of the event, but they won't be carrying wands or pom-poms, given the choice."

Mark looked into my eyes. "Ms. McAllister, do not let me down and tell me you have no plan up your wicked sleeve to combat this."

I batted my eyelashes. "Well, from those on our team that have them, there may also be a posse of cute, doe-eyed under-fives in miniature Forest Hill Ladies footie kits, each holding a pretty little pink beach bucket, wending their winsome way through the crowd with their non-playing daddies."

"You evil bunch!" He snorted. "The guys are dead in the water."

I grinned. "I hope so. I'd love to see them try to run in an evening dress while keeping butterfly-winged diamante specs on their faces if we get to pick Dame Edna for next year's theme."

"Pure evil!" He grinned.

I nodded toward the wardrobe and my shopping bags. "And where better to find a stunning selection of beach buckets for sale than in Brighton?"

Mark let go of his laugh. "You've excused yourself from the office to buy beach buckets?"

I gazed as the shake of his shoulders parted his bathrobe and showed me his chest. I loosened the bow of my wrap. "Maybe not quite just for beach buckets..."

I shrugged my wrap over my shoulders and bared my breasts. His irises darkened. I plucked a foil square from my purse and held it up. "Game on?"

He pulled on the belt of his bathrobe and it fell from him as he stood, his cock hardening. I took my arms out of the sleeves of my wrap and left it on the chair as I darted to the far side of the bed then held out my open hand with the condom resting on it and teased. "Come get?"

I closed my hand over it as he launched himself across the bed and tried for an arm lock around my waist. I saw it coming and danced out of the way. "Uh-uh. Far too obvious a move."

He snaked his hand out and closed it around my wrist. "Or maybe a diversionary tactic." He tugged me closer to the bed and fastened his mouth over the already excited throb between my legs. I whimpered as his tongue probed and I nearly opened my hand when he put one finger then another inside me and stroked. I pulled away, leaped onto his back, held his shoulders then realized my weight was too low to hold him as he flipped me over with ease. He pinned my shoulders and hovered his mouth over my middle to my squeak.

"Mark!"

He gazed into my eyes and licked his lips. "The bout is mine, I believe." I thrashed beneath him as he lowered his head and circled my tummy button with his warm, wet tongue. "Hand it over, Ellie."

I fisted my hand tighter and squealed but lasted only two more minutes as he pressed me to the mattress and explored the sensitive dimple in my center while I squirmed at a sensation so intense as to be near pain. I opened my hand. He plucked the condom from it and named the winner's choice of position as he tore it open.

"Mmmm...your pretty little arse in the air, from behind...over the bed, I think." I bent over, my feet on the floor, my butt raised as he rolled the condom on. He held my hips and eased his cock in.

"Oh, yes..." I sighed.

He pulled back then plunged his cock in harder, his balls slapping between my legs. I pushed back against him and moaned. He increased the pace and the friction built until my orgasm exploded from the center of my mound to race through my belly and thighs.

"Fuck! Yes!" I shouted.

He plunged again and again then groaned his climax. "Ellie..."

We stilled. He withdrew his shaft. I collapsed on the bed and he pulled me into his arms as he lay beside me. "You liked, my little she-dragon?"

I nestled closer and sighed. "Very much."

We lay quiet for a while until his cock softened and he murmured, "I need to use the bathroom."

He put his feet to the floor and took the condom with him. I returned our plates and cutlery to the dinner trolley, turned the television off then used the bathroom after him. I got into bed and snuggled under his arm as he pulled the duvet over us and asked, "Have you set the bedside alarm clock?"

I tucked in tighter. "No. Do you want to set your phone to suit you? Evelynn's keeping her room for the weekend and I'm not expecting to hear so much as a peep from her before lunch."

He smiled and turned out the lights. "It must be a Christmas miracle. I don't have to leave at five-thirty."

I yawned and closed my eyes. "I'd say you'd be more likely to bump into Evelynn if you did."

I woke later in darkness, opened an eye, saw six a.m. so spooned into Mark's back and didn't stir again until he stroked my cheek.

"Ellie, I've got to cut and run. It's past seven and I'm still dressed in yesterday's clothes."

I blinked. "I woke earlier but fell asleep again."

He kissed the top of my head. "Stay asleep. I'll see you at four."

I reached into my handbag standing on the floor beside the bed, swallowed a pill from the packet I retrieved from it, dismissed my pre-set seven-thirty phone alarm then drifted away as the latch clicked on the door. As I'd predicted, my mobile didn't ring with a call from Evelynn until I'd been up, breakfasted, checked out and was shopping in the early afternoon.

"How was the show?" I asked.

"The best! We headed to the most amazing club venue after. I'm running through some notes over a late lunch. Are you still shopping?"

"Yeah, although I'm nearly shopped out. I'll meet you at the hotel around three-thirty."

I carried on shopping and deposited my additional bags with those I'd already left in the care of reception when I'd settled my bill. I saw Evelynn in the lounge, studying a folio of paperwork, fulfilling her reputation as someone who could party all night and still look as sharp the next day as if she'd spent the evening sipping cocoa. I walked toward her and sat in the chair opposite her. "Are there any changes you'd like to make to the running order?"

She shook her head. "Not for me."

I nodded. "Then, as we discussed, I'll give them the good news, hand over the signed authorization and introduce you. When I've said my piece, you give them both barrels and it's your baby from there."

Evelynn glanced at her notes. "Okay. I'll inform them how the scheme will be monitored for the next few months and hopefully put paid to any thoughts anyone might have that I'm a newbie pushover."

I caught her eye with mine. "Sad, but true. You're female and not yet thirty. Get your steely-eyed stare ready and do not give away an inch of niceness."

She nodded. "Thanks, Ellie, for all your help. I feel like I'm good to go."

"I'm sure you are," I said. "Without a legal exec to field any questions, exit the office after you've said your bit. Don't wait for me."

"Have a lovely Christmas, then." She smiled. "Stay in touch? Let me know how it's going for you in your new role?"

"Sure, and you enjoy your Christmas too."

I pushed open the door to Walker and Timpson ten minutes later. We handed over our coats and collected our name badges at the welcome desk. We were escorted to Mark's office rather than the larger conference room. Mark sat behind his desk with his account manager, John, sitting to one side of him and Marjory, his PA, on his other. Evelynn and I sat on the two chairs placed in front of it and Marjory nodded toward the coffee machine bubbling away on a side table.

"Would you like a coffee?"

The smell was divine but I turned it down. "Thank you, no. We won't detain you for too long today."

I opened my attaché case and took out the envelope containing Mark's letter of authorization.

"Good afternoon, gentlemen. After due review and analysis of your independent audit results, I find no further reason to withhold my approval of your scheme."

I put my envelope on Mark's desk as Marjory tapped her fingers, recording my words. "Here is our letter to you confirming the matter, duly signed. This decision will be published on our online information portal in tandem with my previous ruling at such a time as we receive a submission for approval for a product that bears a marked similarity to your own."

I risked a glance at Mark, saw the tilt of his smile then looked at John's broader beam as I clicked my case locks shut. John snatched the envelope off the desk as if he suspected I might change my mind at any moment and take it back. I adjusted my geek specs to sit higher up my nose, fixed my stare on John's face through the clear lenses and said, "So, to the next point on the agenda, namely our monitoring of your compliance with the financial regulations that govern this scheme…"

One small smile and one wider disappeared.

"Today sees the end of my time as a regulator as I move on to take up a new role at the Treasury, so I would like to introduce my replacement, Ms. Evelynn Price. Ms. Price will be the regulator who monitors your compliance going forward."

Mark's eyes widened at the word *Treasury*, as John looked positively gleeful to hear the news that this would be the last he saw of me. I looked at Evelynn and nodded her cue. She sat straighter, opened her case and removed her paperwork from it as I relaxed against my chair back.

"So, gentlemen, as your scheme is a new business model, precedence must continue to be set. I require a second full audit to be completed six months after you launch. Bi-annual reviews to follow it accompanied by, without prior notice, inspections of your financial records by my administration team at such times as I deem appropriate..."

The happiness slipped from John's face as she continued to speak and his expression had arrived at the point of glumness as she finished with, "That concludes my business here today. I will await notice of your launch date."

Evelynn placed her paperwork into her case, shut it and stood. "Thank you for your time, gentlemen." She then acknowledged Marjory with a brief nod and walked out of the office, eyes front.

Mark looked at Marjory. "If you could let me have a printed copy of the minutes when they're ready? And also forward a copy to Ms. Price." Then at John. "We'll start fresh on Monday."

They left the room and Mark looked into my eyes as the office door closed behind them.

"So, Ms. McAllister, the fact that your promotion isn't just upward but also sideways to the Treasury and that

Evelynn is now our regulator sort of slipped your mind last night, did it?"

I met his gaze. "Well, Mr. Walker, I thought I'd best keep a little something in reserve in case you yawned during the meeting because you'd heard it all before."

"Very wise, Ms. McAllister. And to confirm... This does mean you're no longer working at the PRA as a regulator or anything else whatsoever at all?"

I took my phone out of my pocket and the time display showed sixteen-fifty-eight. I laid it on his desk and watched the final minutes click past, then counted down the last few seconds. "Four-three-two-one. No, I'm not."

He laughed. "So, will you risk having a drink with me in the wine bar downstairs?"

I dropped my phone into my jacket pocket and smiled. "Yes, Mr. Walker, I believe I will."

Mark slipped on his suit jacket while I picked up my case. I followed him through his main office, handed my visitor's badge over at the welcome desk and retrieved my coat. He called for the lift and pushed open the door of the wine bar that stood to one side of the entrance lobby, decorated for the festive season by a stunning excess of fairy lights, ordered two gin and tonics and chinked his glass on mine.

"So, the Treasury? What will you be doing?"

"I'm joining the Fiscal Policy Unit as the head of a research team that's being set up to provide statistical analysis and financial projections for the Brexit negotiations. I'll only have a dozen specialist staff reporting to me, so there won't be too much tedious day-to-day admin to complete, thank the Lord."

He smiled then nodded over his shoulder in the direction of a table on the back wall. I followed him to it and put my attaché case beside my chair as I sat. He took the seat opposite me. "Cheers for giving me the lead time before your decisions are published. Will Evelynn stick to it?"

I sipped my drink. "She should. I fairly drummed it into her that it's a big no-no for the Regulatory Office to give the market wind of a new business idea before the concept catches on. I've also linked my two decisions, so the first can't be published without the second. If and when they are, the world and his wife will know that my original query was satisfied and you passed your audit with flying colors."

Mark's phone chirped in his pocket. He took it out, read the screen then asked, "Am I allowed to have your mobile number now?"

I pulled my phone from my pocket. "Sure. It's okay for you to be on my contacts list after today."

I reeled off the digits of my number and he tapped, then I did the same for his and slid my phone into my pocket as he said, "Ellie, do you have to get back tonight? We could—"

His words cut off as the bar door swung open and a woman wearing a thigh-length silver lamé dress tottering on strappy-high-heels with a jacket laid over her arm, stepped through it. Her gaze fixed on Mark and her lips tilted into a delighted smile. She teetered closer—several drinks ahead of our one, going by the sway of her walk and his muttered, "What? No, not now…"

She squealed, "Surprise!" as she reached him.

I thought '*Shit!*' and retrieved my phone from my pocket then looked at the screen and tried for an air of well-occupied.

"I wondered if I might find you in here at this time on a Friday. We've all been *very* naughty and only just left our Christmas lunch do at the Grand. Just *everyone's* going on to the Bubble Bar, so I've come to kidnap you as my plus one."

Her sheet of silky blonde hair whispered across her back as she tipped her head to one side, peeked at Mark beneath the flutter of lowered lashes and wobbled on her shoes. "You'll *love* it! It'll be such fun."

Mark pulled out the chair next to him from the table. "For goodness sake, Angel, sit down before you fall down and make a complete idiot of yourself — and me. I can't believe you've turned up at my workplace in this state."

I dropped my phone into my pocket in readiness to excuse myself from a scene I had no intention of being party to. Angel sat then giggled the amusement of the squiffily, oblivious to what had just been said as she noticed me.

"Hello. Who are you? Do you work for Mark? Don't mind me. I've had a couple, but it's nearly Christmas. You know how it is..."

I looked past her as if she didn't exist, stood and picked up my coat and attaché case. "If you'll excuse me, I think it's time I wasn't here."

Mark reached out his hand. "Ellie, I'm sorry."

I ignored it and shrugged. "No worries. It wasn't you that poured all the booze down her throat. Enjoy your skiing and have a good Christmas."

I stepped away from the table and walked to the door to the sound of Angel's merry laugh. "Didn't she want to come to the Bubble Bar? Oh, well, never mind. She doesn't look much like the type to let her hair down and have a good time, does she?"

Then Mark's, "Oh, bloody hell, Angel! Just put your coat on. I'll pour you into a cab."

Chapter Four

The bar door swung shut behind me and I quick-walked to the hotel, collected my shopping bags, jogged through the town to the station and jumped on the next train to London, replaying the scene from the bar in my head as I traveled. My phone bleeped with a call from Liam. I looked around the nearly empty carriage, put my ear buds in as I answered and kept my voice low.

"Hiya. What gives?"

"I'm ordering Mandy's Christmas present online. It's a leather jacket and quite expensive. If I send you the link, would you give it a look?"

"Sure. Send it through."

"You're very quiet, Ellie. Are you okay?"

"I'm on the train, on my way home from Brighton. It isn't a commuter, so not packed, but still..."

Liam laughed in my ear. "You haven't been there in a while. Met up with your occasional guy while you were about your business, did you?"

"I might have."

He laughed again. "Did you have a good date?"

I huffed down the line. "Yes — then no. I had a drink with him before I came home and another girlfriend of his walked into the bar."

"Oh, bummer," he sympathized. "That'll be bye-bye time from you to him, then?"

"Yeah, probably. I'm okay with other playmates while they're just an indistinct, shadowy someone, but you know what I'm like. Once they have a face, they get in my head and irritate me worse than a pebble in my shoe."

"I'm sorry, Ellie. I know he's not a regular boyfriend as such, but you've been seeing him for more than a year, so you must really like him."

"I do," I admitted. Now free to name names, I added, "And I'll have a go at not turning into a complete bitch because he's also dating Ms. Angel *bloody* Devine, but as I never managed to do so for Luke's Alison or Pete's Natalie, I doubt I will this time."

Liam's voice snorted in my ear. "So, that's why you wanted the place cards changed at the Savoy!"

"Well guessed."

"It's not a name easily forgotten, is it? And sorry again, Ellie, but I copped a good eyeful of her when I was looking around the room for my chance to speak to the minister and she's stunning. If there was ever a name that suited the looks, it's that one."

"Yeah, yeah, a real-life Christmas angel," I huffed. "I'm picturing her now, gracing the top of the tree with the prickly apex branch stuffed where the sun don't shine."

"Ouch!" Liam laughed. "You somewhat more than just like Mark Walker, I'm presuming?"

"Yeah. Unfortunately, I do. I'll see how it goes but I'm not holding my breath. Send the link to me and I'll let you know what I think."

I cut the call and spent the rest of the journey trying not to listen to the worry-worm in my head telling me, *In that state, he'll have had to go in the taxi with her and take her home – and put her to bed. Liam's right. She's stunning… And into him, too…*

The train pulled into London Bridge station and the need for activity put an end to my unwelcome musings. I took the Underground south, turned up the heat in my flat when I opened the front door and dumped my shopping bags beside the sofa. My PJs on with a toasted cheese sandwich inside me and my approval of Mandy's gift sent to Liam, I wrapped the Christmas gifts I'd purchased in Brighton to the noise of the boisterous crowd watching a sport I loved but was totally dreadful at, on the telly – the World Darts competition.

My phone vibrated with an incoming message as I finished wrapping the last of the little extra gifts I'd bought from a shop that sold novelties in The Lanes. I picked it up, saw Mark's name and noted the time, twenty-three-twenty, then tried to ignore the worm as it gave me a picture of him behind a bathroom door texting me while a blonde princess slept the sleep of the well-satisfied in the bedroom outside it, full of booze and sex. I tried to imagine her dribbling and farting in her sleep instead and opened his message.

Are you okay? Can I call you?

I thought about it for less than the minute it took me to acknowledge that if I replied at all, Mark stood to be on the receiving end of personal issues that were mine alone, so I put my phone on the coffee table, ignored his message and took myself off to bed. I looked at my phone in the morning and saw I'd missed a call from him at twenty-three-thirty, followed shortly by a text.

Sorry for the late call if you're asleep. Text or call me in the morning?

I hovered my finger over the call icon, but my head-worm morphed into its full green-eyed hissing persona and obliged with an image of his face in the throes of an orgasm while Angel moaned with pleasure beneath him. I threw my phone into my handbag, growled "Fuck it and damn!" then stomped up the stairs, packed my travel bag and caught the train north at ten.

Mum was waiting as I exited the station. I hugged her and she drove me home. Scampi, his tail on full wag, yipped his delight as I walked through the front door. I received his dog-breath kisses then unpacked my bag of gifts, put them under the Christmas tree and took my travel holdall upstairs to my bedroom. Mum peered into the kitchen cupboard as I returned to the kitchen. "I've got raspberry or the new Earl Grey lemon, if you'd prefer?"

"Thanks, Mum, but straight breakfast tea for me, please."

Mum put our mugs in front of us as she sat beside me at the farmhouse-style table centered through the middle of our large, square kitchen and smiled. "It's lovely to have you home earlier than normal, love. Nana and Granddad will be here in the morning and Aunt Mary and Uncle Fred arrive on Monday, but Uncle Jim and Aunt Rose have booked a Christmas cruise this year, so you won't have to share your bedroom. Beth can have the loft room when she arrives on Wednesday."

I sipped as Mum named my cousin. "Beth's not coming until the twenty-second? That's late for her."

"I know," Mum said. "She couldn't take time off from work any sooner, but at least she arrives the day before Louisa's party, even with it being held earlier this year." She squeezed my hand. "Are you sure you still want to go?"

My face heated and I scowled. "Yes, I am. I'm not staying indoors just because Tim's back in the village. I've got nothing to be ashamed of...unlike him."

Mum squeezed harder. "That's the way, love. Remember your counseling and what the doctor told you. Nature decrees that some pregnancies just aren't viable. No failure. No blame. Tim running off like he did was his decision, his choice and had nothing to do with you."

I nodded, and in the absence of a punching bag, looked at Scampi, asleep in his basket, worn out by the warmth of his welcome to me. "Come along, lazy bones. Get your lead. You and I have got a hot date with several lamp posts."

At the word 'lead', Scampi jumped out of his basket and turned in circles, chasing his tail. I kissed Mum's cheek on my way past her to fetch my parka. "I'll walk him for a while and get my head back into holiday season mode."

I let myself out of the back door and walked with Scampi through our village of one pub, one general store and a sprinkling of picturesque cottages nestled in the scoop of a valley at the head of which sat the larger town of Tinkling Major. I turned my thoughts to anything other than the events of nearly a decade ago as I strode along, but the longer I walked, the more it came to me that by blanking Mark on my phone, I was behaving toward him in the same way that Tim had me.

Our rustic, enclosed bus shelter came into view and I walked into its pitched-pine interior and sat on the bench seat at the back. Scampi stood on his hind legs and put his front paws onto my knees. I lifted him and he settled his rear down on my thighs. I kissed his nose. "I'm acting like a contrary cow, aren't I? When it was me that set the agenda in the first place, not him." Scampi wagged his tail in agreement. "I should let him go, like Jay did me, shouldn't I, if I can't cope with the competition from Angel? Not that I want to…"

Scampi licked my chin in sympathy as Angel arrived in my head, giggling and fluttering her eyelashes at Mark. I gritted my teeth to the flush of my cheeks. "But I'll have to, because I can't."

I walked on and unclicked Scampi's lead as I opened the back door then hung up my coat and sat at the kitchen table. Mum set a glass of wine in front of me and took hers with her as she walked to the range to stir the pot of savory something bubbling on its top. I picked up my phone and dithered as I looked at the screen. *Should I call or text?* I wondered if Mark was home, then whether he might have company if he was, and decided to cool things by text to give notice that my goodbye was in the cards rather than call him out of the blue. I scrolled to his last message, pressed reply and offered him the chance to suggest a convenient window.

Sorry for not getting back to you sooner. I've got a lot on between now and New Year. I'll try and phone you sometime in the next day or so.

My phone vibrated nearly instantly.

Ah…there you are, at last. I was beginning to wonder whether I'd developed phone halitosis or something! Are you as peed-off as me re the wine bar? I really didn't plan on spending my evening drunk-sitting my ex.

I stared at a reply that was in no way the one I was expecting to receive and, more particularly, the last two letters at the end of it. I tapped and sent my question without actually asking it.

Since?

His reply less than two minutes later brought a smile to my face.

Since the moment in my office when you counted down and said, 'No, I'm not.' You? The guy from the Savoy?

My heart thumped. I re-read his message to make sure I hadn't mistaken its meaning, then hissed *'Yessss'*.

Mum's head swiveled toward me. "What you got? A good score on Candy Crush or something?"

I smiled and flicked my hair over my shoulder. "Maybe, but I'm not playing Candy Crush."

She laughed and I tapped back.

Liam. My mate from uni and the opposition's number 10. If you didn't spot my name on the seating plan, it was because I was listed as Amanda aka Mandy, his girlfriend who came down with a stinking cold and couldn't go with him.

I wondered why I didn't, but the table plan was gone when I tried to look at it again after I saw you. Mmmm... I think it's time I broke some of the rules we play by. Watch for me, my little she-dragon. I'm coming for you.

My breath caught as it raced through me how much I wished he would. I looked at his message again then replied with my opening move.

Yeah, yeah, yeah. You gotta catch me first.

Mmmm...sweet. Challenge accepted. Game on, Ellie.

I giggled at my phone and Mum looked at me. "Okay. I won't ask who or what is putting the sparkle in your eyes. Set the table and call your dad, will you? Supper's ready."

I stood, opened the cutlery drawer, laid three places settings on the table and hollered, "Dad...supper."

Once we'd eaten, I phoned Liam to see whether Mandy's jacket had been delivered and Lucy for a progress report on the arrangements for the charity match. Scampi jumped up and curled beside me on the sofa as I cut the call and I laughed my way through Geraldine eating the same Christmas lunch over and over again during a re-run of an episode of *The Vicar of Dibley* alongside my mum and dad then took a mug of hot chocolate up to bed.

* * * *

The next morning, Nana and Granddad arrived and I threw myself into the festivities, making sweet mince pies, mixing eggnog with more brandy in it than the recipe asked for and picking up the Christmas cards every time a door opened and the subsequent draft lifted them from the mantlepiece and dropped them to the floor. After lunch, in line with my refusal to stay out of sight indoors, I took Scampi for a walk and summoned every bit of pride I possessed to greet everyone I met with cheerful unconcern, despite the speculation I knew would be running through the village grapevine.

In the evening, GIFs started arriving as direct messages on my previously Mark-free Facebook page—a puppy with its tongue hanging out performing a begging trick, a hand offering and re-offering a bunch of red roses, another hand rolling and re-rolling a pair of dice. For each one I received, I sent one back—a dog chasing after its ball, a sneezing hay fever animation, a dark-haired woman rolling her eyes and mouthing, 'yeah, yeah, bring it on'.

My aunt and uncle arrived in time for supper the following day and, after we'd eaten, the possibility of an amble to the pub was raised. Aunt Mary looked at me. "Your mum says *he's* finally come home to visit his mother, and much as I'd like to give him a mouthful, how do you want to play this?"

I chose my words carefully. "That I made my feelings known at Sebastian's funeral will have the village agog at the prospect of me giving them a repeat performance, so if I see Tim, I'm going to steer clear and behave as if I haven't and I hope he'll act the same way toward me."

Aunt Mary nodded and speared a pointed look toward Dad, then Granddad and, finally, Uncle Fred. "Message understood? Disinterested ignoring is the order of the day."

I couldn't help but smile at the protective huffs and puffs as they nodded their agreement while I reached for my parka. I zipped it up and stepped outside into newly-arrived-from-the-Arctic gusts of swirling wind. Dad pushed open the door to the Harvest Home fifteen minutes later and I put down my hood, more relieved than I would ever admit to see no sign of a stocky, black-haired male as I took off my coat and glanced around the room.

Louisa spotted me and ran over. "Hey, Ellie. Where's Beth?"

I hugged her. "Hiya, nearly birthday girl. Beth's not home until the twenty-second."

Louisa smiled. "So long as you're here and she's on her way. Come and have a look. I'm just putting the finishing touches to the buffet menu with Aaron."

I put my hand in hers and she pulled me toward the bar. Aaron set a gin and tonic on it and I offered him my cheek as I picked it up. "No rest for the wicked when you come home, as usual, I see."

At any other time a solicitor in Bristol, Aaron pecked me back. "Absolutely not for those whose parents own the local pub. How are you, Ellie? You're looking good."

I smiled and sipped. "And you." My phone vibrated in the back pocket of my jeans. I pulled it out and snorted as I opened a Facebook message from Mark to see an animation of Santa, his face planted between the thighs of one of his elfettes, his head bobbing up and down. I giggled and replied.

Mr. Walker. Pack it in. I'm in a pub full of peeps looking over my shoulder!

He sent me a pic of a fire-breathing dragon.

Don't care. Smoochies. Xx

Which made me laugh so much I nearly spat out the next mouthful of my drink. I replaced my phone in my pocket and watched Aaron walk to the other side of the bar and begin to restock the fridge with bottled soft drinks. Louisa watched him too then nudged my arm. "So, while it's just us, I could make it clear to you-know-who that he isn't welcome, if you'd like."

I shook my head. "Thanks, but no. That would hurt Lorraine, and I wouldn't wish that on his mum when she's never been anything other than fine to me. There'll be no drama to spoil your party if he's here, not from me or any of the McAllister clan."

Louisa puffed out then smiled. "Cheers, Ellie. It's fantastic that everyone attends because of my birthday being on Christmas Day, but it's grown into such an event over the years that I'd feel awful if anyone didn't have a good time. It's all so overwhelming compared to the kids' afternoon tea party with a magician or a bouncy castle and ice-cream it started out as."

I noted the worry lines creasing between her eyes. "Stop the parties, then, if they're proving to be more of a hassle than they're worth."

She nodded. "I'm moving that way. Of the original squad, we're all in our late twenties and early thirties now, and I think it might be time to get over the concept that I'm in some way missing out because I was born on the twenty-fifth of December."

I flicked my gaze around the bar. "It must cost you a fair bit to put it on, but I don't think the pub will suffer if you decide to spend your cash elsewhere on a celebratory spa break or something. Everyone will still turn out because it's Christmas."

Louisa offered me her fist. I bumped it with mine and she said, "I agree. I won't say anything before the event, but I'm going to make this the last one. Although, in saying that, I'm now going to enjoy it to the hilt because it's my final hoorah, and if you want to knee Tim in the groin, I'll cheer you on."

I laughed. "I have no intention of providing the evening's entertainment, thank you. I'll ignore him if he turns up, as I think he will me. We haven't spoken in nearly ten years and I don't suppose he's come home for Christmas because he's bursting for us to have a chat."

Dad walked up behind me as I put my glass on the bar. "Louisa, the menu looks great. Ellie, are you ready to walk back?"

I smiled. "Sure."

I blew Louisa and Aaron a kiss and followed Mum and Dad out of the pub, with Nana and Granddad alongside Aunt Mary and Uncle John gossiping behind us.

"Pad Thai, well, really!"

"I've never heard of food like that being served at the Harvest Home."

"That's city food, that is, although I expect it will taste the same as last year's chow mein."

"Or maybe like the tagliatelle of the year before…"

Mum caught my eye with hers as we passed under a streetlight and we exchanged smiles at Nana's and Granddad's aversion to any dinner that didn't include a helping of potatoes soaked in brown gravy. Dad let us in through the back door and I took a mug of hot chocolate up to bed then laughed out loud at a GIF of an elfette poising a pair of big, licky lips over Santa's erect cock as I climbed under the covers.

* * * *

The next morning the Arctic blast was accompanied by some flurries of snow, so in the afternoon, after a long soak in the luxury of a hot bath, I dressed in my last year's joke Christmas present, a fluffy poodle onesie, complete with ears and a tail that looked ridiculous but was thick and warm against icy drafts. I sat at the kitchen table with my nail file to prepare them to be ready for false tips and an application of Christmas sparkle the next day and my phone vibrated. I picked it up to see a text from Mark.

Are you home? Can we chat?

Sure. I'm in. Call if you want to.

Okay. Speak shortly.

I put my phone down and waited for it to ring. Nana, wrapping a gift farther up the table, looked up. "Smiling at your phone again, Ellie? Is there someone special on there?"

"A friend that sends me jokes, Nana."

Mum lifted one of her one-pot wonders out of the oven and stood it on the worktop. "There…that's ready for everyone when they're hungry."

The doorbell rang as she added a loaf of crusted bread and the butter dish to stand beside it.

"That's early for Beth, isn't it?" Nana said.

Mum closed the curtains over five o'clock early evening darkness as she walked past them to answer the front door. "Perhaps she's looked at the weather forecast and come early. It's starting to snow again."

I applied my nail file as I waited for Mark's call then heard his voice.

"Oh, hi. I'm sorry to bother you but I saw your house lights were on. My car's broken down and my phone's out of battery. I wondered… Do you have a landline I could use to make a quick call to my breakdown recovery service?"

"Goodness! What a day for such a thing to happen," Mum replied. "Come along in. It's freezing out there. The phone's there on the hall table. Come through to the kitchen when you're done."

My heart thumped and my face heated as I looked down at my furry bedsuit. I debated the possibility of ducking out of sight under the table and its draped linen covering, with no chance of running upstairs to change my outfit with Mark in the hall, as Mum walked into the kitchen. "Shame! That poor man's car has broken down and his phone's out of charge."

I carried on with my manicure with a silently shrugged, *Oh, well, what you see is what you get.*

Mark's voice ceased. He walked into the kitchen with a suitable expression of surprise pasted onto his face — possibly made easier to achieve by Scampi dancing around his ankles and yipping in doggy delight at an unrecognized human scent.

I met his eyes as he said, "Ellie? Is this your parents' place?"

I swallowed an urge to snort at his ham acting and added a little of my own. "Wow! Yes. Who would have believed it? You've broken down outside my mum and dad's."

"Is this a friend of yours, Ellie?" Mum asked.

"Yes, Mum…from work," I said, and did the honors. "Mark, my mother Betty and my grandmother Joan."

He smiled. "Pleased to meet you."

"Well, fancy that." Mum smiled back at him. "Sit you down. I daresay you've got time for a hot drink. The breakdown service will take at least an hour to get to you, I expect."

He sat on the chair beside mine. "Thank you. At least that, they said. I'm on my way to spend the holidays with a friend and took the back road to avoid the Christmas congestion on the main route."

Nana picked up her wrapped gift. "I'll just pop this under the Christmas tree and see if Bill's ready for a cuppa."

Mark leaned closer as Mum turned away to fill the kettle. "So, my little she-dragon-turned-pooch, are you cool with my being here or are you going to growl and chase me off?"

I gazed into his eyes and tried to keep my delight that he was here out of my own. "An outrageously underhanded opening maneuver, Mr. Walker. I take it there's nothing wrong with your car?"

He gazed back. "Nope, not a thing…nor my phone."

I ran my fingertip along his jawline. "We're cool."

His face relaxed. "Good. When my breakdown service arrives, I'll apologize when the car ignition fires right up."

Mum turned toward us. "Milk and sugar, Mark?"

"Milk, no sugar. Thank you, Betty. You're *very* kind."

I nudged his leg and muttered, "Careful on the saccharine there."

"I thought I was being winsomely cute. Too much?" he muttered back.

"I'm going to have to ask for the barf bag if you keep it up."

"Damn!"

Mum set two mugs of tea in front of us as the back door opened and Dad and Beth walked in. Dad put down Beth's suitcase. "Look who I've found. Her car was stuck behind old McGregor's veg-picking outfit. His tractor hit an ice patch, jackknifed from its trailer and blocked one end of the road into the village."

Dad paused as he noticed Mark then looked at Mum.

"This is Mark. His car broke down, so he came here to use the phone and it turns out that he's also a friend of Ellie's who she knows from work," she explained.

Dad held out his hand. "Pleased to meet you, Mark."

Mark offered his own and shook. "And you, Mr. McAllister."

Dad smiled. "It's Mike."

Beth walked forward—a cousin I adored but one to whom the words 'engage brain before opening mouth' had never applied.

"Hello, Mark, I'm Beth. Well done there, our Ellie... although I'm not sure the doggy suit is exactly what I'd be wearing if I was dressing to impress." She shrugged off her coat and looked at her luggage. "Aunty Betty, am I sharing a room with Ellie?"

"No. You've escaped this year." Mum smiled. "You're in the attic room and away from her snores."

"Mum!" I said.

Beth giggled. "Well, you do, Ellie."

Mark whispered in my ear with everyone's focus still on Beth, "I call them little sleep puffs myself." I swatted his arm as the phone rang in the hall and Mum walked out to answer it. She looked at Mark as she came back.

"That was your breakdown company. There's been a pile-up on the motorway. They said sorry, but they'll be another couple of hours yet. Not to worry, though. I've cooked a one-pot-enough-for-everyone dinner. Will you stay?"

Mark smiled his thanks as the back door opened and Aunt Mary and Uncle Fred walked in, shaking snow from their shoulders.

"The snow's settling. Only an inch so far, but we decided we'd best get back from the pub," Uncle Fred said.

Aunty Mary kissed Beth. "Hello, poppet. You're here earlier than Dad and I expected."

Beth introduced Mark to them as 'Ellie's friend'. Mum lifted the pot from the work surface onto the table and added the bread board, butter, plates and cutlery as Nana and Granddad took their places. I passed Mark a side plate.

He leaned closer. "Ellie, I'm sorry. I didn't mean to intrude like this. I only meant to call in and see you for a short while."

I smiled. "Don't worry. My mother is at her happiest cooking for a full table and an unexpected guest will do nothing but make her day."

Dad cut slices from the loaf and Mum ladled onto plates from the pot. Beth picked up her fork and asked,

"I didn't get the call, so who's been nominated to buy the joke present this year?"

I raised my hand. "I can't say I didn't have to do a little extra gift wrapping this year."

"Oh good Lord no!" Granddad spluttered. "Ellie, if it's underpants that light up again, I'm not wearing them."

"But, Granddad, you only had to wear them over your trousers," I countered.

Granddad looked at Mark. "They not only lit up but also played a Christmas carol when they did."

Beth laughed. "But, Granddad, Rudolph the big boy reindeer had a—"

"Beth, don't remind me, please."

Mum stacked the plates when we'd finished eating. Uncle John took them over to the dishwasher and parted the curtains. "Blimey, it's an absolute blizzard out there now. Snow shovels at the ready in the morning, folks. It looks to be several inches deep already."

I looked at Mark then tapped for a traffic report on my phone. "We're on lockdown for vehicle access in or out of the village. The veg-picker's still blocking one end of the road and someone's misjudged the steepness of the hill and flipped their car at the other end."

"Is there a hotel nearby?" he asked.

"The pub has a few rooms for bed and breakfast guests. I'll ring them."

The landline rang in the hall and Mum called Mark's name as I spoke to Aaron at the pub.

"Your breakdown service to say they can't get to you?" I guessed as he retook his seat. He nodded, so I reassured him. "The pub has a room free. I've told them to expect you."

Mark thanked Mum for supper and I walked him to our front door. He pulled me toward him. I wrapped my arms around his neck and tilted my face for his kiss. He pressed me close and nuzzled his lips into my hair after our mouths parted. "I want to take you sailing and watch you play football, Ellie, to spend lazy Sunday mornings in bed together — for it to be you and me. No one else."

I held on tight, breathed the scent of him in and kissed his neck, then stepped back and fixed him with my best regulatory look. "In that case, Mr. Walker, take care as you walk to the pub. And text me to say you're okay when you get there — and cancel your callout. Come back here after breakfast so we can discover a loose lead to your battery and miraculously start your car."

He grinned and hugged me to him. "Yes, my little she-dragon."

I kissed his cheek then opened the front door. "Turn right and walk until you see the village green. The Harvest Home is on the far side of it. You'll be pretty soggy by the time you've waded through the white stuff."

"I've got an overnight travel bag in the car that I packed to use at Larry's. I'll grab it and my boots." He stepped outside and was lost to my sight after only a few paces.

I returned to the kitchen and wiped the stupid grin off my face as I opened the door. Mum poured tea and we adjourned to the sitting room with the biscuit barrel and a mug each and watched an old recording of *The Muppet Christmas Carol*, to ramp up our Christmas spirit. Mark's text lit up my phone screen halfway through it.

Arrived at the pub and, as you said, soaked through. But the room's good and the shower hot. Mine hosts are very kind. I ordered a pot of coffee and they added a large brandy to the tray 'to keep out the cold'.

Yes, they are. I went to school with their son Aaron if you see him around in the morning. See you after breakfast when you're ready.

I went to bed at the end credits of the film and pictured Mark, less than half a mile down the road, as I laid my head on my pillow then closed my eyes with a contented sigh at the thought that we could now be together without me having to keep looking over my shoulder.

Chapter Five

I woke in the morning and looked out of the window to see a scene that could have graced any Christmas card, but not one I'd want to drive through in anything other than a four-by-four. After breakfast, I slotted my feet into fleece-lined Wellington's, zipped up my parka and we all trooped outside to shovel snow, spread salt and create a walkable path, with every household in the village doing the same to ensure we at least had pedestrian access to one another.

Mark arrived, dressed in his ski-jacket with jeans tucked into Timberland boots, as I joined my freshly shoveled section of path to Uncle Fred's. "You're well organized. I thought I might have to wade through the snow to get here, but the pathways have been cleared all the way."

I leaned on my shovel and puffed. "We get a couple of bouts of this every year. It's not like in the south where anything more than a flake or two is a rarity."

"Can I give you a hand?" he asked.

I smiled. "We're just about done. Let's get the snow off your car. Did you cancel your breakdown callout?"

He nodded and walked to a low-slung, snow-covered hump. "They sounded pretty relieved. They're dealing with incidents on the main roads as a priority."

I joined him. "We can start it, but I don't think you'll be going anywhere until the snow plough's been through."

"That's what I thought when I saw the depth of the fall. I don't need to get to Larry's until the morning, so I booked another night at the pub, just in case."

"The plough will clear the A road first, but it should be through sometime today."

Mark grabbed hold of my hand, tugged me closer and stuffed a handful of snow inside the collar of my coat. "Are you keen to get rid of me already, Ms. McAllister?"

I squealed as icy rivulets trickled down my back, took a handful of snow from the roof of his car, lobbed it at him and missed.

He laughed. "No chance."

I eyed him up and down. "I can wait. Revenge will be mine."

He grinned, clicked his key fob to disengage the motion-sensor alarm and I started to swipe thick, soft snow from the window and driver's door while he did the same to the front and cleared the sport-nose of the car. I opened the door. "Do you want to fire it up or fiddle?"

He threw me his key fob. "For the sake of my manly pride, you start it and I'll fiddle. The bonnet release is under the steering wheel to the right."

I jumped into the driver's seat, located and pulled the lever then gave him a couple of minutes to poke around in the engine before I put the key in the ignition and called, "Ready?" He stood straighter and nodded. I checked that the gear shift was in neutral, depressed the clutch and turned the key. The engine roared to life with the deep throatiness of its high-performance, sports-model pedigree.

I let it idle while Mark closed the bonnet and Dad called from farther up the road, "Oh, well done. You fixed it. What was it?"

I cut the engine.

"Nothing really, with daylight to be able to see it. Just a dodgy connection to the battery terminal, so no charge was going to the alternator."

I got out of the car as he walked around it, offered him his key and took my chance to scoop up a handful of snow behind his back while he pushed the car door shut then plunged my hand past the waistband of his jeans, leaving my icy revenge in the crack of his butt.

He gasped as Mum called, "Coffee's up in here."

I giggled, danced out of reach of any retaliation and fist-pumped the air. "Howzzat for a Brucie Bonus? You also get to drink your coffee in wet underwear!"

"Evil woman." He snorted.

I waited for him to catch up to me and gave him my best witch's cackle. "Revenge is sweet."

He smiled, took off his glove and offered me his hand. "Walk to the pub and have lunch with me after?" I nodded and put my hand in his. He tucked both of our hands into his jacket pocket. "Your hand's freezing."

I put my other in my parka pocket. "I know, but I couldn't shovel properly in my mittens."

I led Mark around the back of the house and opened the door to the kitchen after we stamped the snow from our feet on the hairy bristle mat outside it. A tray of assorted mugs filled with steaming coffee, along with the sugar bowl and cream jug, stood on the table.

"Help yourselves," Mum said when she saw us.

We draped our jackets over the backs of two chairs and sat opposite Beth, a mug standing in front of her. She surveyed the tips of her fingers then opened her mouth wider than the Mersey Tunnel. "I'm glad we got the snow cleared without a chip on my varnish. What are you wearing to the party tonight, Ellie? Something short and clingy to give Tim the middle finger if he turns up, I hope."

I kicked her shin under the table. "I don't suppose I would even recognize him after all these years."

Beth's eyes watered but for once she'd got the message. "Yeah...true."

Mark looked at me. "Your party is tonight, not tomorrow?"

I nodded. "Yeah. Louisa's mum has a houseful staying this year, so she moved it forward to give her mum a day's grace before Christmas Day. Do you want to come with, if you're staying on at the pub?"

He smiled. "Ms. McAllister, are you attempting to kidnap me as your plus one?"

I gazed. "Do you want me to?"

"Yeah." He gazed back.

"Then, yeah."

Beth snorted. "Don't be such a goofball, Ellie. There's no avoiding the party if you're staying at the pub."

Nana walked into the kitchen and swiped Beth's shoulder as she walked past. "I heard that, Elizabeth Ann. Manners, please. You ask, not assume."

I poked the tip of my tongue out at Beth, put my mug on the table and stood. "Lunch, Mark?" She returned the gesture as Mark placed his mug alongside mine and

I called to Mum, "Back later. I'm walking to the pub with Mark."

"Okay, love. See you soon."

I picked up my purse and fastened my coat. Mark followed me to the kitchen door and offered me his hand when we reached the cleared path. I took my mittens from my pocket, put them on and placed my hand in his.

He lifted both our hands and looked at the hand-knitted pattern of miniature Christmas puddings dotted over my bright scarlet mitt. "Very seasonal, and made by?"

"My mum," I said. "The year before last's joke present. We all received a pair and had to eat our Christmas lunch wearing them. Only trying to use a knife and fork in my boxing gloves could have been worse."

He laughed. "And what treat have you got lined up for them this year?"

"Mustaches," I announced. "All different and luxuriantly hairy. I found them in one of those shops that sells weird and wonderful things down The Lanes."

"But your dad already has a 'tache."

"Yep. So, his is the most extravagant handlebar job, so wide it'll tickle his ears."

"Well, that should cover the real one when it's stuck on."

I laughed. "You think I'm going to let them get away with sticking them on? You know I'm not that nice. They have a clip that pinches onto either side of your nostrils, and anyone found not wearing their hairy attachment from the time they receive it until the time they go to bed will have to dip their fingers into my little box of forfeits."

He snorted. "Send me some pics Christmas Day when you're all wearing them?"

"Sure," I said. "What will your Christmas Day be like? Party, party?"

Mark stopped walking and pulled me toward him. "I won't let Larry down, but mine will be spent wishing deeper snow had kept me here."

I put my arms around his neck and urged his face closer. "Take me to bed?"

He nibbled my bottom lip. "Just the lunch offer I was hoping for." I hugged him to me, kissed him hard full on his lips and didn't care who saw me do so.

We walked on and arrived at the pub. Mark pushed open the door into the small lobby with its half-glass door that opened onto the bar and restaurant to the right, a solid door hiding the stairs to the upper floor on the left and, between the two, a welcome desk with a small office behind it. I slipped around the unoccupied desk. "What room number?"

"Four."

I released the catch to the wall cupboard, removed his key on its chunky wooden fob and offered it to him. "Ex-chambermaid's inside knowledge, my holiday job from fourteen until I was old enough to work behind the bar."

Mark opened the door to the stairs and I followed him upward to the next floor. He unlocked the door to his room and I saw it hadn't been altered since I had last cleaned it, with shades of lemon-and-cream sprigged flowers on the curtains and matching counterpane and the furniture old but polished to a high sheen. I dropped my purse onto the table beside the bed, unzipped my coat and laid it on the armchair as he relocked the door. He added his coat to mine and put his arms around me. I lifted my face for his kiss and pressed closer as I tasted his mouth, and he cupped my butt and kissed me deeper.

I stepped backward and sat on the side of the bed then took off my boots and socks, shrugged off my jeans and pulled my thermal tee over my head. Mark mirrored my movements then walked toward me naked, his cock hard, glistening with lubrication. I removed my underwear and lay back on the pillow, moved into his arms as he lay beside me and pressed my breasts against his chest as we kissed. He squeezed and fastened his mouth over my nipple when our mouths parted. I threaded my fingers through the back of his hair and arched my back for more. He sucked my other breast, pinching then tugging on the nipple he'd set free, and the sensation raced around my groin. Wet and wanting, I felt for my purse, dipped my fingers into it and offered him the condom without suggestion of bed games.

He covered his shaft, kissed my lips, stroked between my legs, teased me open with his fingers and eased his cockhead in to my sighed, "Oh…yes."

He pushed deeper and my breath caught in the back of my throat as he filled me. I wrapped my legs around his thighs and rocked against him. He thrust faster. I moaned as his cock pummeled inside me, cupped the globes of his butt cheeks and squeezed as I raised my pelvis to meet his. He increased the pace. I arched my back to the increased throb of my clit when he pushed my breast up to his mouth and my climax pulsed out as I writhed beneath him.

"Fuck, fuck!"

He sucked harder and his thrusts shortened to his groaned, "Yes…"

I eased my legs down as we stilled then lay drowsy in the afterglow until he pulled out of me, knotted the condom and stroked his fingertips down my cheek with a soft kiss on my lips.

"Do I need a little history lesson before tonight, Ellie? About Tim?"

I replied with a small shake of my head. "Not really. It's ancient history as far as I'm concerned. The village can hold its collective breath if he's at the party, but they and he will get no reaction from me."

He gazed his question into my eyes. "Tell me about him anyway?"

I gazed back and knew that if I wanted any deeper relationship with him, Sebastian was someone he needed to know about. I wrinkled my nose.

"I will, but it's a toughie. Everyone in the village already knows the back story and Tim's not a subject I talk about if I can help it."

He stroked down my back. "Would a large gin and tonic make it easier?"

I nodded. "Yeah, I think it might."

He reached for his jeans. "I'll go to the bar and bring up a couple."

I re-dressed then sat cross-legged on the bed and tried to arrange the words in my head while he was gone. Mark handed me my drink after he'd let himself into the room and I took a healthy swig as he joined me on the bed. He sat with his back resting against the headboard and prompted, "So…Tim?"

I chugged another large glug. "Um… Okay… I think perhaps I should start with the person it's all about really…Sebastian."

I swallowed hard as I said my baby's name then took a deep breath and headed straight to the heart of the matter. "So, when I was seventeen I gave birth to Sebastian."

Mark's eyes widened as his mouth formed the silent question I'd guessed it would — *'A baby?'*

I held on tighter to my glass and spoke the words that hurt the most. "But Sebastian was premature and he died a few days after he was born. Tim is Sebastian's father."

I paused and gulped down another mouthful as Mark held my hand. "Bloody hell, Ellie. I'm sorry."

I smiled a small smile and carried on. "Tim had stood by me and was committed to taking his share in raising Sebastian. He was at the birth and by my side afterward until the day of the funeral, when he didn't bother to show up. His mother was beside herself thinking his car must have crashed on its way to the chapel, but when she got back to their house, it was to find he'd packed all his gear and legged it back to uni instead of following her to the funeral, as he'd said he would. He wouldn't answer my calls or respond to my emails asking why, then he blocked me from his social media and phone and I've neither seen nor heard from him since."

"Oh, fuck!" Mark said.

I raised my glass. "Exactly. Sebastian's funeral wasn't a private affair and I'm afraid I fell apart in a fairly spectacular fashion. It was the first and last time I'll ever do so in public, but most of the people who witnessed it will be at the party."

A distinctive chugging sounded outside. I looked at Mark and offered him his excuse. "That's the snow plough. You could be at Larry's by seven-ish if you head out now."

He pulled me closer. "Ellie McAllister, pack it in or I'm going to have to bite you all over."

I relaxed against him. "I'm just saying that tonight is my personal shit-fest, so if you'd prefer to cut and run, I'm cool with that."

He took my glass from my hand, stood it on the bedside table with his and wrapped his arms around me. "I'm going nowhere, Ellie. I've wanted to be more involved with you from the first time you came to my hotel room. It's you that kept me at arm's length."

I hugged him to me, sat straighter, then said what I'd never admitted out loud to anyone other than my counselor and my mum. "Losing Sebastian messed with my head and left me in a pretty dark place. I blamed myself for not being able to carry him to term. I was a loser, a failure and someone Tim could no longer bear the sight of because he thought so too. I had counseling but what really brought me through was restarting my studies. I'd missed quite a chunk of the school year and had a lot of extra work to do to catch up, so I spent every waking hour studying. I passed all my exams with barely a mark dropped."

"And that made you feel okay about yourself again?"

"It was the beginning. Getting those top grades reassured me that I had value. Setting goals and being successful at work is how I make sure I stay feeling that way. I'm protective over my career because it keeps the darkness where it belongs—in the past. I don't ever want to feel that hopeless again."

Mark kissed my hair. "I would never have guessed, not any of it."

I lifted my face and kissed his lips. "No, I'm naturally ambitious and competitive. That particular year aside, I always have been. My method couldn't work for me otherwise."

He rubbed the tip of his nose against mine. "Game, set and equally matched on that score then."

Having cross-referenced eight years of his annual accounts, I acknowledged the drive that must have been required to grow a company from ten staff at inception to the hundred-plus he employed now. "I think you might be winning the race on that one."

He smiled. "Nah. All I'm up on you is a few years' head start."

I puckered him an air-kiss for the compliment then looked at the window to see dusk closing in. "I'd best get going. Party time here in the sticks begins early."

Mark sat straighter. "I'd better see what emails I've got. John's working right up until close of business Christmas Eve on the detail of the IT software specification we need to run the new scheme."

I put my feet on the floor and picked up my boots. "Poor John. He looked so delighted to see the back of me until Evelynn opened her mouth."

"I know," he agreed. "Are we okay to talk shop now?"

I nodded. "Yeah. I'll keep it quiet that we're involved when I start my new job until the ink's dry on your authorization, but apart from that, for any use I can be without violating my security vetting, I'm team Walker and Timpson from here on in."

Mark fist-pumped the air and I asked, "Is there a Mr. Timpson or is it just a name you use to lengthen your letterhead? I ordered copies of your previously filed year-end accounts from Companies House when I was reviewing your audit and didn't catch so much as a sniff of him."

"I'm glad to hear there are some things that escape regulatory reach." He smiled. "Albert Timpson's my grandfather and he loaned me the start-up money I used to form the company."

I put my nose in the air and sniffed as I picked up my purse and coat. "I believe I was checking your financial records at Companies House, not those of your family tree at Somerset House, Mr. Walker." I leaned over the bed and kissed him. "I'll text you when we leave the house. The women do the full works and dress for the occasion. The guys wear jeans with a collared shirt, although if we girls are lucky, also their Sunday boots and not their Wellingtons. The dab of cow pat behind each ear is optional. There'll be plenty of hot food. See you this evening."

He laughed. "*Eau de ruminant.* I think I'll pass, thanks. See you soon."

I blew a kiss over my shoulder as I walked out of the room and stepped up the pace against a darkening sky as I let myself out of the pub door.

The kitchen was empty when I opened the back door and walked in. I poked my head into the sitting room and saw everyone, apart from Beth, watching the television. "I'm going to make a start on getting ready."

Mum nodded. "Beth's already doing the same."

I walked up the stairs as Beth stepped through the bathroom door with a towel wrapped around her body and another around her hair. She hustled me toward my bedroom. "Right, you. Spit it out. Who is he? More than just a work *friend*, I think."

I sat on the side of my bed. "Yeah, Mark's more than that. We've been friends with benefits for a while but we're ready to step it up now and only date each other."

Beth grinned, flicked her hip and shimmied her butt. "Oh, yay. Oh, yay…"

I raised my eyes with a smile until she added, "And he's drop-dead-gorgeous enough to give Tim a right royal up-yours if he sees you all glammed up and standing beside him."

I shook my head. "No, thanks. I won't deny that how Tim behaved after Sebastian died still pisses me off, but I don't have any personal feelings left for him that would make me want that type of reaction. I'll be dressed to the nines for the party because we always do. I'll be with Mark because, by chance, he happens to be staying at the pub."

Beth waved an airy hand and danced out of the room. "Very noble of you, cuz. Although if Tim turns up, I personally will be watching his face when he catches sight of you and realizes exactly what he let slip through his fingers."

"I haven't changed that much," I called after her.

"Oh, yes, you have," she tossed over her shoulder as she disappeared around the turn in the attic stairs.

I tutted, without meaning it, in remembrance of my coltishly-awkward teenage self. I used the bathroom, dried my hair, clipped it back as I had at the Savoy and completed my look with silver-gray, smoky eyes, false lashes and plenty of black under-liner. Cherry-red and strapless, my dress had a boned bodice that didn't require a bra, so I rolled silken, lace-top hold-ups over my legs, stepped into the dress then started to apply glitter varnish to my natural nails, too short on time to attach extensions.

A half-hour later, Mum called up the stairs. "Ellie? Beth? Get down here. You must be ready by now!"

I loaded my evening clutch, rolled leggings and a long but thin jersey-knit top into a neat sausage around my toothbrush, slipped my feet into high-heeled black courts and walked down the stairs to the kitchen.

Granddad popped the cork on a bottle of fizz as I walked in and he spluttered, "Ellie! I'm not sure that dress is even decent."

Beth pranced into the kitchen behind me as I stowed my sausage into the pocket of my parka, her dress as figure-emphasizing as mine and a little shorter. "Don't be daft, Granddad. The girls always *bring it* to the party."

Nana sent the ghost of a wink toward me. "If you've got it, flaunt it. I always did."

Granddad smirked at her and poured. Aunt Mary and Uncle Fred walked into the kitchen and we all picked up a glass, toasted each other and sipped. I put my glass down empty, sent Mark a text then zipped up my coat. Dad told Scampi to 'stay', opened the back door and I followed Beth out. Mum grasped my arm and held me back, so we were the last pair in our torch-lit two-by-two procession.

"Ah…Mark? Pure coincidence it was our front door he knocked on, was it?"

I smiled. "Not quite. He wanted so see me, so yeah, he made up an excuse to call in on his way to spend Christmas with his mate. Don't let on?"

Mum squeezed my arm. "Of course not."

I glanced sideways at her. "I won't be home tonight."

She nodded and we walked a little faster to catch up with those ahead. Beth pushed open the lobby door to the Harvest Home. I followed her in, hung up my coat and Dad opened the door to the bar. I lingered so I could say hi to Mark after he'd been deluged by my family. I waited for the calls of "Evening. How are you doing?" to die away, then stepped through and took in the stretch of his shirt over the width of his shoulders, along with the snug fit of his jeans as I sauntered toward him.

I brushed my lips against his cheek when I reached him. He rested his hand on the small of my back and kissed under my ear. "Drooling. You look gorgeous, Ellie."

I pressed closer. "You look beautifully edible yourself, Mr. Walker." Music sounded as the deejay fired up the sound system in the restaurant-turned-party room next door.

Mark passed me a drink and I perched my butt on the bar stool beside his. Beth, arm in arm with Louisa, joined us and I introduced him to the birthday girl. Aaron put the empty punch bowl on the bar and asked Louisa as he tipped in a bottle of red wine, "What do you reckon? Brandy or rum in this one?"

"What was in the last one?" she said.

Aaron grinned. "For a head-start, both."

Louisa smirked. "Why change a winning formula?"

Aaron smiled, unscrewed a bottle of brandy and poured. Two more of Tickling High's former inmates, with their partners, walked in through the door to Louisa's cry of welcome. "What time do you call this? Get over here, you slackers!"

Scott and his fiancée, Rosie, alongside Russell and his husband, Ian, arrived at the bar. Aaron dipped a ladle into the punch and filled several glasses then picked up the bowl and took it to the party room as more of the village piled in through the pub door. I told Mark the names of those arriving at the bar as more alumni of Tinkling High crowded around us and their families joined the tables of neighbors and friends already seated. The noise level rose as drinks were ordered.

Louisa called above the hubbub, "I've reserved us some tables in the other room." My ex-sixth-form squad turned to follow her. I swung around on my stool to face the bar and Mark did the same.

"You don't want to join them?" he asked.

I signed to Aaron's dad, Ray, for a couple of refills. "No. Polite disinterest works best from a distance. I always intended to sit with family rather than friends tonight." I reached for my purse as Ray set our glasses down in front of us and Mark placed his hand over mine.

"Uh- uh. No way. You're a tab up on me from the hotel last week." Ray nodded at him, rang the price of the drinks through the till and put the receipt on the shelf behind the bar to be added to Mark's bill.

Dad and Granddad walked up behind us and ordered three pints of ale. Mark motioned to Ray that he would buy the round. Granddad drank the top off his beer and licked the foam from his top lip.

"Cheers, lad. That's better. The punch is all very well for the ladies, but I can't take more than a glass of it."

Dad smiled his thanks at Mark then said, "Ellie, we've saved a couple of seats for you at the table."

I nodded. "Okay. We'll come through when the buffet is open."

Alma Nutley, our nearest neighbor, pushed up to the bar on her wheeled walking frame. Ray poured a large schooner of sherry and set it on the bar then put her till receipt into an empty glass for Dad to settle her tab, as he always did.

Alma looked at me. "You're looking well, my duck. And sitting with that nice young man you were kissin' earlier today, I see."

I bit my bottom lip to stop myself laughing and Granddad picked up her glass. "Come along, lass. I'll carry this through for you."

"Lass!" she cackled happily. "Bill McAllister, you always did have a wicked way with you! It's no wonder you managed to snatch Joan from under the noses of the others that were looking her way."

Dad smiled as she trundled off with Granddad one step behind her. "Be grateful for small mercies, love. At least she put in her false teeth tonight."

I let out a giggle as he walked away with his and Uncle Fred's pint glasses of dark beer, one in each hand.

"Does she often appear without her teeth?" Mark asked.

I smiled. "Alma's a poppet but thinks of her teeth like other people would a piece of jewelry — precious and only to be worn on special occasions. Tonight counts, but I won't be so lucky when she comes to our house for Christmas tea. Trifle followed by Dundee cake she can dip in her sherry to soften do not call for the inclusion of teeth."

He grinned. "Pics or it ain't true!"

"Coming your way. Just don't look at them if your own meal is looming on the horizon."

He picked up my hand and kissed the pulse of my wrist. "I'd rather have seen it for real."

I stroked my fingertips along his jawline and voiced a hope that wild horses couldn't have dragged from me a few days earlier. "Maybe next year?"

He smiled. "For definite next year."

I gazed and contemplated giving in to my urge to pull him closer and snog his face off until Ray cleared his throat and rattled a plastic box full of discarded beer tops to call our attention to our empty glasses. I looked away to the flush of my cheeks and Mark's. "Thanks. A refill would be good."

The ice cubes rattled in my drink as Ray set it down on the bar. I stiffened as the room quietened behind me to give me notice of who had just walked in.

Mark threaded his fingers through mine. "You okay?"

I forced my shoulders to relax, changed the subject and kept my voice bright. "Sure. What time is your flight tomorrow?"

He smiled his understanding into my eyes as he answered. "Just after one, but I've told Larry I'll go direct to the airport and meet him there, so I don't need to be on the road until around eleven."

I fixed my attention only on him to the sound of Ray's voice. "Evening, Lorraine. Nice to see you. Haven't seen you in a good while, lad."

I asked, "Isn't that cutting it a bit fine? The airport's an hour's drive from here." Mark gave me his flirtatious wink and I tutted with a small huff as I got it and said, "You're turning left to the upper-class seats when you get on the plane, aren't you?"

His smile widened. "Yep. This is my first vacation since this time last year. It's only short haul. I am *so* not turning right."

I raised my nose in the air and sniffed. "Priority boarding? Valet parking? Meet and greet?"

He nodded. "Absolutely…and when I fly home on the thirtieth."

"The day of my charity footie match."

"I'll come and find you as soon as I can, then we could stay over at yours?"

Heady with my freedom to accept, I didn't hesitate. "I'd like that."

He raised our linked hands and kissed into my palm. "Come home to my place after? Let's see the New Year in together."

A ripple shivered through me. "Yeah…"

A soft cough behind us interrupted. I glanced over my shoulder then turned sideways when I saw it had emitted from Tim's mum.

"Hello, Lorraine. How are you?"

"Fine, thank you, Ellie. You're looking very well yourself."

"Thank you."

Her gaze flickered toward Mark then returned to me. "Perhaps we could have a little chat somewhere quieter than the bar?"

I shook my head. "Sorry, but no. That would create unnecessary drama and that's not on my 'to do' list tonight. Just let it go and I will too."

Lorraine agreed with a short nod, and I added as she turned away, "I'd appreciate it if that message was passed on." She nodded again, and I could nearly hear a disappointed sigh as she walked off when I faced front.

I picked up my glass and Mark asked softly, "His mother?"

I nodded and murmured, "Look over my shoulder. Is there a dark-haired, stocky bloke with her?"

He glanced. "Stocky, yes. Dark-haired? Might have been before it headed west and he shaved his head."

I tried to picture it and failed but resisted the urge to turn and see for myself. On the other side of the bar,

Aaron began to pull corks from bottles of wine and gave us the heads-up. "I'll get a bottle of red and white on each table then Mum will open the buffet."

I sipped the end of my drink. "Thanks. We'll go through."

I picked up my clutch, stood and turned in the direction of the party room without so much as glancing at any other occupant of the bar. Mark rested his hand in the small of my back and I moved my hip closer to his.

"You must be hungry? You missed lunch," I noted.

He clasped my waist. "I'll take more of that kind of lunch any and every time."

I looked sideways. "Supper first, then we could exit stage left, point made."

He smiled. "With the bottle of fizz I still owe you?"

I breathed, "Yes, please."

Dad was turning empty wine glasses right way up on the table when we reached it then poured a selection of red and white. "Pinot Grigio or merlot? Take your pick."

I selected a red, Mark the same and we sat on the vacant chairs between Nana and Aunt Mary. I put my bag on the table and swept my gaze around the room as I took a sip. To my left, the squad had gathered around three tables that had been pushed together near the deejay. Running down the length of the room opposite me were tables seating four or six, and it was on the fifth one along that I caught my first sight of Tim sitting with his mother and two of her also-widowed friends from the Ladies Afternoon Tea Club.

I moved my gaze straight on past him and my cheeks heated as it occurred to me that if Mark hadn't told me about his shaven scalp, I would have embarrassed

113

myself with a goggle-eyed double-take at the difference the lack of hair had made to his face. I gripped my glass tighter and pictured red rivulets running down it as I stalked over and tipped its contents over his head, until Mark's soft squeeze on my free hand recalled me. "Your aunt was just wondering how long we'd been working together."

I looked at the gleam of mischief lighting his eyes and turned our hands so I could see his wristwatch.

"About three hours, I should say, wouldn't you?"

He grinned.

I looked at Aunt Mary and explained. "We've never worked together, as such. We just move in the same work circles…"

Beth appeared at my shoulder and crouched so her mouth was level with my ear. "Oi, you. I sent you a vid. Didn't you get it?"

I opened my clutch and didn't see my phone. "Damn! I must have put my mobile in my coat pocket, not in my bag, when we left home." I stood. "I'll just go grab it. Back in two."

Beth slid onto my chair. I walked to the lobby and saw at least a couple of dozen coats and jackets had been added to the rack since I'd deposited mine, so I searched beneath those covering it on the peg I'd used and found it missing. I searched farther along the rack before it occurred to me that on other occasions when the rack had become overfull, additional space had been made by removing the contents of a couple of pegs to the desk in the office. I looked over my shoulder, saw the pile then the distinctive fur edging of my parka hood in its midst, so walked into the office and heard Tim's voice as I reached for my coat.

"I nearly didn't recognize you, Ellie."

I froze for an instant then turned on my heel and rued my lack of a glass of wine as I looked into cool, gray eyes regarding with me as much dislike as I was sure my own face was returning in spades. "Then why do so when I made it clear to your mother that I'd rather you didn't?"

"So she said, but that's not good enough. There's something I need to know first-hand."

I noted the fixed set of his jaw, recognized the expression as one he wore when determined to have his say and my hackles rose. "You bugger off without so much as a word then think it's okay to reappear ten years later and make demands of me, do you?"

He ignored my question and carried on, regardless. "I got married a couple of years ago. Mum wants me to bring my wife here for a visit. I need to know how things stand. I don't want to say no to her, but I won't do it if what happened between us is still going to be following me around."

My blood pressure heightened at the lack of even one word of regret.

"So, let me get this straight. You feel no need to apologize for behaving like an absolute *shit*, but you hope all is forgiven and forgotten by now?"

He tutted his impatience. "Oh, come along, Ellie. Surely, enough time has gone past for you to have got over it by now."

The word '*it*' grated and I clenched my teeth. "Are you referring to our son, Tim? If so, use the name you gave him."

He raised his eyes heavenward. "Oh, for God's sake... And people wonder why I legged it? I could see all this coming my way—the soul-searching, the tears, you clinging onto me, never letting it go..."

My heart raced to a thundering pounding in my veins as the word '*it*' came out of his mouth again, and my intention to maintain a distant, calm façade fled. I toed off my shoes, fisted my hand and put everything I had behind my shot as I stepped forward and swung for him. My right hook connected with a satisfying crunch. He rocked on his feet and my following left-handed uppercut smacked his head against the doorframe to my snarl.

"Wrong answer."

He slumped to the floor holding his face. "You hit me! You fuckin' well hit me…"

I looked at the blood leaking from his nose and growled. "Yeah, and you eff'n well deserved it. Your head's so far up your own arse it's meeting tomorrow's lunch coming the other way! Now, take my message on board. Stay away from me and I will you. End of!"

I turned my back to him, retrieved my phone and heard, "And if *I* come across the slightest whisper that you haven't just slipped and hurt yourself on your own account, *I* will find you and dust you down a little more. Comprendez?"

I swung around and saw Mark towering over Tim, looking at him like he was something that had just crawled out of an open sewer. I stepped up into my shoes and took Mark's offered hand with my phone clasped in the other. He looked at our linked hands and my reddened knuckles as we walked away.

"We saw him follow you out, so Beth showed me the vid on her phone. I thought I'd best come see what was going on. You're going to need ice."

I felt the hot throb from the power of my uppercut made without gloves. "Yeah…but *damn*, it felt *good!*"

He lifted my hand to his lips and kissed. "Your hand is going straight in the ice bucket when the fizz comes out of it."

I smiled, threaded my arm through his, and we walked to the party room to see the McAllister table tucking in to their supper. Mark filled a plate with spiced pad Thai noodles while I filled another with a selection of Asian accompaniments, some of which belonged to Thai cuisine and some, like onion bhajis, which didn't.

We sat and put our sharing plates on the table beside Beth, who'd captured a spare chair and wriggled it in beside ours. I bit into a samosa, happy to find that the subdued light in the room hid the redness of my knuckles, as she leaned closer and muttered, "Well?" I picked up my phone and opened her video message. From the angle, I guessed she'd shot it through the open door of the party room.

She nudged my arm. "I told you I'd be watching."

Her phone cam zoomed in on the bar. Mark and I sat at it with our backs to the lens. We turned to face each other and Tim's face came into focus. He looked in my direction then stared and his eyes widened before his gaze moved to Mark and his expression changed to one of chagrined anger as he turned away. I put my phone on the table and picked up a piece of sesame prawn toast to Beth's whispered, "So, what was all that about?"

I shrugged. "He's pissed off because he'd like to bring his wife to the village and the fact that he can't or won't is all down to me, apparently."

Beth gaped. "Fuck! What's he on?"

Beth's expletive attracted Nana's glance and raised eyebrows in our direction. I nudged Beth's knee with mine. "Shush. Eat." She filled her mouth with noodles while I offered Mark a bite of my prawn toast and watched Aaron speaking into Lorraine's ear. She picked up her handbag and hurried from the room.

Aaron walked closer, reached over my shoulder and picked up our empty red wine bottle. "Someone lost their footing and slipped on a patch of black ice when they stepped outside for a breath of fresh air just now. They bashed their face something rotten when they fell. Lorraine's gone home to administer the necessary first-aid."

I looked at him wide-eyed. "Really? Oh well. Never mind. Accidents do 'appen."

Beth snorted and choked on her mouthful as she swallowed.

I patted her back. "Easy there, cuz."

Aaron chuckled. "I'll bring you a fresh bottle."

I picked up my fork, twirled it through the fast-cooling noodles and managed three mouthfuls before I gave up and settled for a couple of duck pancakes while I sipped my wine. Mark soldiered on until two-thirds of the portion was gone, while across the table Granddad huffed at his plate.

"How the hell are you supposed to keep the slippery little buggers from sliding off your fork?"

Mum laughed. "Don't worry, Dad. I left a pan of Scotch broth ready to be heated through for you and Mum when we get home."

Granddad's face brightened. "Joan, did you hear that? Our lass has done us a bit of real grub for later."

Mum caught my eye with a smile as Nana laid her cutlery on her plate with a puff of relief.

Mark murmured in my ear. "Real grub?"

I leaned closer. "Proper dinner contains potato and meat gravy."

He smiled. "Fish and chips?"

"Lunch, not dinner."

"Cold meat and salad?"

"Lunch, not dinner."

"Pizza. Lunch not dinner?"

I shook my head. "Foreign muck — and not real food at all."

He laughed. "And when abroad? Or don't they travel?"

"They like to cruise where the onboard chefs are very obliging to their passengers' preferences if notified in advance at time of booking."

Mark grinned and sipped his wine. I passed our plates onward to be added to the stack farther up the table. Sophie, Aaron's sixteen-year-old-cousin, hefted the pile and took them to the kitchen as the deejay cranked up the volume of the music. Several of the squad headed to the center of the dance floor while Granddad offered Nana his hand and they began an elegant quick-step while managing to avoid those throwing their shapes with more abandon to Cameo's *Word Up*. Beth joined the throng and I rested the throb of my hand against the chill of the white wine bottle as I watched the dance floor fill.

Mark looked. "Point made? Ice time?"

I dropped my phone into my clutch and nodded. "Yeah, please. If you want to organize the ice, I'll drop a word in Mum's shell-like."

We stood. Mark headed to the bar while I leaned over Mum's shoulder and whispered close to her ear, "No fuss, I'm disappearing now. See you in the morning." She nodded. I straightened and went to join him.

Chapter Six

A bottle of champagne was standing in an ice bucket on the bar and Aaron, polishing a glass flute with a linen cloth, smirked at me when I reached it.

"I take it you're joining us for breakfast?"

I thought of the menu item the kitchen most dreaded being ordered.

"Yeah, I'll take the Eggs Benedict — warm yolk, firm white, crispy rashers, no lumps in the Hollandaise." I looked at Mark. "What do you reckon? An out-of-season fresh berry salad to follow?"

Mark nodded and named two fruits nearly impossible to obtain even when 'in season'. "With white currants and loganberries?"

Aaron laughed and pushed the champagne forward. "Yeah, right. That'll be two full English then, with an extra slice of fried bread if you're lucky."

I blew him a kiss as I took the glasses and Mark the ice bucket. We exited stage left through the half-glass door. I scooped up my parka from the office desk on my way through the lobby then followed Mark up the stairs. He pulled his room key from the back pocket of his jeans and unlocked the door. I dropped my coat onto the chair then put my clutch and the glasses on the bedside table. He released the cork and poured, took the napkin from the neck of the bottle, scooped ice into it, sat on the side of the bed and patted his thigh. My left hand throbbed with heat, so I sat, laid it palm down on his leg and picked up my glass with my other hand. He placed the ice pack over my knuckles. "Red and bruised but you haven't broken the skin. How do you feel?"

"My hand or me?"

"You."

I sipped my fizz and considered the matter. "Justified. More at peace now that I know the reason why he ran, even though I will loathe him forever for the lack of respect he showed his son by not turning up at the chapel."

"And showed to you."

I emptied my glass. Mark topped it up and I drank a mouthful.

"It certainly made my situation worse. If he couldn't face the emotional fallout from me but had left after the funeral with even a few words of explanation for his mum to pass on, it would have been a young-love, just-for-the-summer relationship that ended unhappily but would have been true history by now."

Mark removed the ice pack, lifted my hand, contemplated the result then added fresh ice to the napkin and replaced it. "How'd it go down in the first place?"

I took a large swig of my drink and allowed memories I normally repressed to float into my mind. "A baking hot summer day, larking around in the lake. In swimwear, barely dressed. He was supposed to pull out…then couldn't."

Mark frowned. "Bloody hell, Ellie. He should have known better than to go down that road if he'd already done a year or two at uni."

I shrugged. "As should I. I'd had all my year twelve personal health education lectures at school. The free samples they hand out were in my bedside drawer."

He lifted the ice pack and looked into my eyes. "It was your first time, wasn't it?"

My cheeks heated. "Yes. So? That doesn't excuse me from being a total dickhead."

He replaced the napkin. "Hmmm…. I think you and I might have to agree to differ on that point."

"Maybe, but I was over the age of consent and I'll stand by my actions, as I did when I refused a termination once the consequences became clear."

"Did he ask you to have one?"

"No. Tim supported my decision not to abort what was, as far as we knew at the time, a perfectly viable life for no other reason than we'd made a mistake. Most of my friends thought I was certifiable but I knew my family would do everything they could to help me look after a baby. That made it a lifestyle choice to me and I couldn't go there."

Mark tossed down a mouthful of wine. "Thankfully, it's not a discussion I've ever had to have."

I sipped mine. "Or one I ever intend to have again. I'm uber-careful with my pill. I take it first thing so I know it's done for the day and I've got an Alarmy app on my phone to make sure there's no chance I'll sleep past the time when I should take it."

"Alarmy? I've not heard of that."

I put my glass down beside my bag, removed my cooled hand from under the ice pack, took my phone out and tapped on the app. A photo of my contraceptive pill blister pack came on screen with a dismiss icon below it and I turned my phone toward Mark. "The world's most irritating alarm. You take a pic and the alarm will only stop when it receives the same pic again. I can cancel if I wake before it sounds at seven-thirty, but once it does, I can tap the dismiss icon all I like and my phone won't give up trilling until I actually move my butt and snap the matching photo."

"Fiendish." He smiled. "No chance of forgetting to take the thing with that around."

His swift glug of wine and the word *thankfully* resonated in my mind. "Has someone forgotten on you?"

He drank another mouthful and rested his glass beside mine. "Yeah, Laura. We'd been seeing each other for a year or so when I caught sight of her pill pack and there was a day here, there and the other that hadn't been popped. She laughed it off, said she'd been busy and had forgotten to take them, but there was something about her reply, along with a couple of other things she'd said, that seemed off to me and I couldn't get it out of my head that she was playing Russian Roulette with them."

"Shit! No! What did you do?"

"Bought a box of Durex and haven't had sex with her or anyone else without wearing one since."

"Snap. One time only for me. Neither have I since Tim."

Mark cupped my chin and kissed my lips. "But now that we're an 'us'?"

I gazed and my body came alive with the desire to feel him inside me, skin on skin. I shoved past history back where it belonged, and, for the first time, rested my trust solely on my pill as I murmured, "I want it to be just us, nothing in between."

He pulled me into his arms and put his trust in me. "I want that too."

I lifted my face and deepened our kiss, unbuttoning his shirt as I explored his mouth.

He pulled on my zip but the boned bodice that held my breasts securely in place wouldn't open unless I was upright and straight, so I stood, released it and stepped out of my dress. The rise and fall of Mark's chest increased as he moved his gaze to my breasts, lower to my pussy, over my gartered thighs, down the extended length of my stockinged legs perched atop my high-heels, and growled. "Jesus, Ellie..."

I looked at his bulging crotch and licked my lips. "You have a little fetish for high heels and stockings, Mr. Walker?"

He unzipped his jeans, pushed them down and off then cupped my butt and urged my pussy closer to his face. "I do now." He stroked the bare flesh above my stocking-top then licked and sucked my mound. My excitement built as he teased my swollen clit with his tongue and I pushed him backward onto the bed, pinned his hands, straddled his waist and offered my nipple to his lips. He drew it into his mouth. I lifted my hips and brushed my wetness over the warm tip of his uncovered cock. He released my breast with a soft moan.

"Ellie, take me?"

I let go of his hands, sat straighter, eased the head of his cock in then sank lower until his shaft was deep inside me. I sighed with pleasure at the difference the absence of a condom made. I rocked back and forth, slow and languorous, savoring the sensation of his warm, not so slickly smooth cock, and purred. "Oh…yes. That feels good."

He grasped my butt. "So, good, sweetheart…to feel you on me."

His words rippled down my spine and I rocked faster to the urge of his hands. He breathed harder, his gaze fixed on my bouncing breasts as I ground down, panting. He grasped them, one in each hand, squeezed to my moans of appreciation and I climaxed as he pinched and extended my nipples to the shortened thrusts of his orgasm.

"Oh, God, Ellie… Yes…"

I laid my head on his chest, still impaled on his cock, and listened to the rapid beat of his heart beneath my cheek. He held me close while it slowed then I eased away, curled into his side and felt a slight trickle between my thighs. "Oooh…sticky."

He put his arm around me and smiled. "Good sticky?"

I snuggled closer and kissed his shoulder. "Very good sticky."

We lay quiet and listened to the hubbub outside as people called their goodnights to each other as they left the pub to make their way home. He kissed into my hair. "I like this, being able to spend the night together without it being anybody else's business but ours."

I nuzzled into his neck. "And me. Do you want to use the bathroom first or me?"

"You go. I can wait."

I took my toothbrush from my coat pocket on my way and Mark swapped places with me after I'd finished.

We cuddled close and he switched off the bedside lamp. I sighed with contentment, closed my eyes and checked the time on my phone when I woke to see that it was still dark.

Mark stirred as the screen brightened. "How close to the evil alarm?" The time display showed six-fifty-five, so I reset the alarm for the following day and reached for my pill. "Close enough. Nearing seven." I swallowed then snuggled under the duvet.

Mark wrapped his arms around me and spooned into my back. I wriggled my butt against his groin. His cock stirred, so I wriggled again. He tightened his arms around me and kissed my shoulder.

"You wanting something from me?" he asked.

My pussy wettened in anticipation of early morning sex and the feel of his stiffening erection on my back. "Yeah."

I tilted my head for his lips on my neck. He kissed, stroked his fingertips down my belly and explored my aroused pussy.

I sighed as he slid his fingers inside me and asked, "You need my cock in here?"

I mewled and lifted my leg for him to enter me from behind.

He withdrew his fingers and replaced them with his warm cockhead. I whimpered my pleasure as his hardness filled me and I pushed back against him as he murmured, "Beautiful, to feel you wet on me." He thrust faster.

I moved his hand to my breast. He squeezed, kneaded and pinched my nipple. I rotated my hips, panting, his hard shaft thrusting inside me, the throb in my clit pulsing, near climax, to his voice soft beside my ear. "Yes, sweetheart. Come on me."

I moaned. "Bite." He sank his teeth into my shoulder and my orgasm ripped through my groin in a wet tidal wave as Mark groaned his final climax to my yell. "Fuck! Fuck!"

Aftershocks spread through my pelvis and I whimpered with the joy of them as we stilled. I turned into his arms and he held me tight to him until we could speak again, then he kissed my lips.

"It's just as well that I'm the only guest on this floor at the moment, I think."

I giggled. "Don't care. Smoochies."

He flicked the duvet off us and swatted my bum. "Up, you, and get in that shower. Man needing his breakfast here."

I tutted and swung my legs off the bed. "Cheeky! I'm sure early morning butt swiping is my job."

He laughed. "Ha! Not anymore."

I poked the tip of my tongue out at him, flicked my hair over my shoulder and pranced off to the bathroom.

Showered, I dressed in my leggings and top, put my party clothes in Mark's holdall, slotted my feet into my courts and followed him downstairs. I called "Good morning" through the kitchen door to let whoever was on duty know we were there. We sat at the only table laid with breakfast place settings in the restored-to-normal-order restaurant. Aaron's mum, Beryl, bustled out, took our order and soon returned with toast, coffee and two plates of lush-smelling fried food.

I tucked in, hungry, having eaten not much more than three forkfuls of noodles the evening before and I cleared my plate excepting the slice of black pudding, which I'd never had a taste for. Mark ate everything on his and I poured myself a second cup of coffee while he returned to the room for his travel bag and my coat then settled his bill. He tucked the receipt into his wallet after he handed me my parka and zipped up his jacket.

"It always takes me aback how reasonable the prices are in the north compared to at home. A large gin and tonic costing less than a fiver... I can't remember the last time I paid less than a tenner in Brighton."

"It's a shocker," I agreed. "They're that at the clubhouse and it's a subsidized bar. Fourteen quid a go at the pub nearest my flat. It's no wonder pre-drink parties are the norm in the south."

I slipped my arm through his and called to Aaron, who was restocking shelves in the bar, as we walked through it, "Bye. Happy Christmas for tomorrow."

Aaron called back without looking up, "And you. Have a great day."

I looked again and couldn't help but wonder why my normally laid-back mate was looking a little sheepish and not meeting my eyes. Mark opened the street door of the pub. I put my hand in his and he walked me home. Mum and Nana were sitting at the kitchen table peeling sprouts when we stepped into the kitchen.

Mark handed me my folded dress with my stockings tucked inside it and Mum and Nana wished him a safe trip and a Happy Christmas. He thanked them then I walked him to his car. He stowed his holdall inside it, pulled me close and I hugged him to me for our goodbye kiss.

I nuzzled into his neck as we broke apart. "Have a good flight. Text me to say you've arrived okay and message me while you're there. And have a great time — but not *that* great. I'll see you on the thirtieth."

He laughed. "Yes, my little she-dragon. I'll be counting the days."

I smiled and let him go. He got behind the wheel, fired up the engine and my heart climbed on board and went along for the ride as I watched him drive away.

I walked back into the house when I'd lost sight of his car, hung up my coat and blew a kiss in the direction of Mum and Nana as I picked up my party clothes.

"I'll take these up."

Beth was sleeping quietly on the top floor and my bed looked so tempting that I undressed, slipped under my duvet and slept for more than a couple of hours. The sound of the shower running woke me and I used the bathroom after Beth then walked downstairs to find Mum, Nana and Aunt Mary admiring an arrangement of Christmas roses, greenery and candles that had obviously just been delivered. I asked, "Who sent it?"

Mum held out the gift card. I took it and read.

It was lovely to meet you all. Thank you for making me welcome. Mark.

I smiled and handed it back. "He didn't tell me. He must have done an online order while he was waiting to board at the airport."

"It's beautiful and very kind of him. Pass on our thanks, will you, when you next speak to him?"

I nodded, took my laptop from the dresser shelf, searched for Mark's hotel and, as I hoped, found it to be a sizable, high-end complex. I scrolled down a list of its retail outlets and a chocolatier offering 'individually hand-crafted' items caught my eye. I clicked and filled in the order form to commission a single dark chocolate in the shape of a mustache. Then, hoping he was the only guest of that name since I didn't have a room number to give them, paid an eye-watering number of

Swiss francs for it to be created and delivered to him in the morning.

I closed my laptop after receiving my e-receipt and called to Scampi, "Lead." Beth walked into the kitchen as he twirled in circles and I zipped up my coat.

"Wait for me. I'll come," she called.

I held Scampi outside the kitchen door as she put on her boots and jacket then we set off down the drive. She waited until we were clear of the house before she asked, "So, last night? Tim. What was all that shit about a wife?"

I considered how much detail I wanted to confide and found the mention of Tim's name didn't heat my temper now that I'd had my say and given him an almighty thump, but also that I didn't much care if word got out that I had, so I didn't dodge her question.

"Tim said the reason he left in the first place was because I was over-emotional after losing Sebastian and he didn't want to be around a clingy mess that couldn't let go."

Beth goggled at me and I carried on. "He married a couple of years ago and thought enough time had gone by for me to have gotten over *it*, as he wants to bring his wife here to visit Lorraine but won't without my reassurance that everything is forgiven and forgotten now."

"The cold-hearted bastard!" she spluttered. "Mum always said that Lorraine wrapping her life around him after his dad died would make him a spoiled, self-centered brat. I hope you bloody well put him straight!"

I nodded with satisfaction at the memory. "I friggin' well punched his lights out."

Scampi yelped his surprise as Beth fist-pumped the air and yelled, "Yesssss!"

I picked him up and scratched behind his ears to soothe him as she laughed.

"So, he didn't slip on black ice?"

I kissed Scampi on his nose. "Nope. What he slipped on was my fist then Mark's offer to add to it if he made a fuss over the matter."

She grinned. "You and Mark are both obviously goofy over each other. What took so long?"

I stood Scampi on his feet. "Work. We shouldn't have been seeing each other at all, but—"

"Now that you've got a new job you can," she guessed and offered me her hand to high-five.

I slapped her hand and noticed sparkles of light dancing in her eyes, far too bright to be just happiness on my behalf. I remembered Aaron's earlier sheepishness in the pub. "Oh, yeah, you. What are you holding back? Cough it."

She laughed and twirled in circles as exuberant as any Scampi could manage. "Well, maybe at last Aaron might have noticed that I'm not fifteen anymore and the six-year age gap between us doesn't matter now that we're in our twenties."

I grinned at her open delight. "You didn't go home last night either, did you?"

She danced away with a giggle and called over her shoulder as she began to run. "No. We were in room two and close enough to hear—"

I tugged on Scampi's lead and chased after her. "You ever let that one out of your mouth and I'm going to kill you!"

We arrived at the kitchen door laughing and breathless. Scampi collapsed in his basket when we walked in. We hung up our coats as Mum spooned portions of cottage pie onto plates for our supper, and after it, we all adjourned to the sitting room to watch a feature-length episode of Christmas *Gogglebox*.

Mark's text of *Arrived and checked into the hotel okay* arrived halfway through it, accompanied by a video of the sparkling winter wonderland he'd shot from his room balcony with the words *Deffo Christmas here*.

I pointed my phone at the lights twinkling on our Christmas tree then around the room to capture the laughs and snorts of everyone watching Giles and Mary on the telly. His answer pinged onto my phone two minutes later.

Wish I was there or you were here. xx

I smiled at the kisses and messaged back.

Wish too. xx Was the flight good? Champers all the way?

Yep. Unlimited Moët, tho I only had 2 glasses and the lighter sushi lunch option. I was still so stuffed from breakfast. Larry did somewhat better and is still being the life and soul of the party going on in the bar downstairs while I've snuck up here for a nightcap from the mini-bar.

Lol. No alcohol for me today as it'll be a heavy day tomorrow. Mimosa at breakfast, wine at lunch, sherry with Alma at five and an open bar while we play silly games in the evening.

Downturned sulky mouth. I want to be playing silly games too. Especially with you, sweetheart. xx

I gazed at the same endearment that had thrilled me when I'd heard it in bed but hadn't managed to return it, so breathed in deep and let it out.

Want too, darling. So much. xx

Whoa, my lovely she-dragon. Did you just say the 'd' word to me?

I smiled at my phone.

I might have.

I love you. xxx

I silently squeed as my heart lifted on a cloud of fairy dust then danced to the tune of a magical unicorn, and I tapped back,

I love you too. xxx Now drink your drink and enjoy yourself, but not too much. And I will talk to you tomorrow when Santa has been.

Mark's reply pinged less than a minute later.

He just has. xxx

My skin goosebumped to my mad grin at my phone screen. I looked up to see if anyone had noticed and saw an equally inane expression plastered over Beth's face as her thumbs worked on her handset. I took the small cushion from behind my back and threw it at her head. She gasped when it scored a direct hit and volleyed it back at me to our dads' reprimands.

"Ellie..."

"Beth..."

Nana intervened by lobbing her own well-aimed cushion at them with a screech worthy of Noddy Holder. "It'sss Christmaaa…ssss!"

Mum laughed, pressed the remote and turned off the television. "Nearly, but not quite. Get up to bed, the lot of you. I want you all sitting around the breakfast table by seven sharp in the morning. No excuses."

We all laughed at the same admonishment she gave us every year then trooped up the stairs. I pulled the duvet around my neck as I lay down and hugged my pillow in place of the man I wished it was, savoring his words of love as I drifted off to sleep with a satisfied smile on my lips that it was me he wanted and not the Christmas tree topper, no matter how stunningly pretty she was.

Chapter Seven

I woke in the morning before dawn to the magic of Christmas Day, the world outside still coated with the black of night, the inside of our home illuminated by the twinkle of fairy lights that had been left switched on while we'd slept. The murmur of voices reached me from below, so I threw my pill down my throat, zipped myself into my poodle suit then wandered downstairs to see if I was the last to arrive and found I was.

Mum looked at the fictional watch on her wrist. "About time too."

I kissed her cheek on my way to my seat. "Happy Christmas, everyone."

She smiled as I sat to the shout of 'Happy Christmas' from the rest of the table. Uncle John popped a cork and Granddad stood. "Unaccustomed as I am —"

We all groaned without meaning it. Uncle John half-filled the glasses, topped them with orange juice and Granddad raised his.

"To the McAllister clan, past, present and those still to join us. Happy Christmas. And to those no longer with us... Absent friends."

We stood, as we did every year, lifted our glasses and intoned the response for all those gone from us that we loved and missed. "Absent friends."

I retook my seat, the smell of roasting meat floating on the air with our enormous turkey and equally large joint of gammon ham already in the oven to cook through in time for our Christmas lunch that would be served promptly at one, so as to be eaten in time for us to watch the Queen's live broadcast to the nation on the television at three.

Mum passed a basket of croissants around the table, along with a bowl of fruit salad and another of yogurt standing in the middle of it for those that wanted it — our Christmas breakfast designed not to overfill our stomachs and spoil our lunch. I cleared the table and washed the dishes afterward, alongside Beth, while we waited our turn to use the bathroom. Nana and Aunt Mary swapped places with us and began to dress the table in its Christmas finery while Mum opened the oven door and gave the meats their first of many bastings.

My phone vibrated on my dressing table as I zipped up my jeans, and I opened a picture message from Mark to see him lying on his bed, dressed in blue salopettes and a thermal tee, his satisfyingly large chocolate mustache carefully balanced under his nose.

Hey, look what one of Santa's little helpers just brought me! (although it's going to end up smeared all over my face if I wear it much longer!) Thank you, sweetheart. Happy Christmas. xx

Lol, then you are excused from my little box of forfeits! (although Mmmm…lickable melted chocolate!) Happy Christmas, darling. xx You just about to head out to the slopes? It's pressie time here, so I'm just about to dish out the hairy versions.

Mmmm…lickable sharing when I get home then! And yep, the conditions here are perfect, so the skiing should be good. I don't know if I'll get a phone signal on the runs but I'll try and send some pics. Send me loads of your day? xx

Yeah, please and sure. Have fun. xx

And you. xx

I smiled, put my phone in the back pocket of my jeans and floated down the stairs. Grandad handed me a glass of sparkling wine when I walked into the sitting room then Dad passed out the presents sitting beneath the tree. Our gifts to each other being treats more than extravagance, I looked at my haul of fluffy socks, PJs, perfume and shower products then watched my 'little extra' gifts being unwrapped with accompanying flinches as they were attached to nose nostrils. I pulled a tissue from my pocket and let them off the hook. "Pad the clip."

Beth ripped a piece from my hand, did as I suggested then laughed. "You are such a wind-up merchant!"

I attached my own 'spaghetti western' drooping 'tache, took my phone from my pocket, sent Mark a selfie then pics of all those in the room as they did the same. I followed it with several more pics I snapped throughout the morning, along with a video of Mum downing a shot of sprout cooking water when her 'tache fell off and Uncle John hopping a circuit of the sitting room on one leg after he'd removed his 'Ronald Coleman' to snooze after we'd watched the Queen.

Alma stirred us from our after-lunch stupor when she arrived shortly before five. Mum and Aunt Mary pushed Great-Grandma's double-tiered hostess trolley into the sitting room laden with Christmas tea and my phone vibrated as the trifle was dished. I looked at the screen, saw Mark requesting FaceTime so excused myself to go and sit on the stairs and take his call. His face didn't fill the screen when I answered but the real-life version of the person I'd seen in stills of a similar trip a year ago did.

"Hello, Larry. Where is he?"

Larry grinned at me, his eyes over-brightly happy. "He gave me his phone to film his last run of the day, so I've hijacked it. He'll kill me, but I've had a shitload of schnapps and wanted to say hi because he's mentioned you several more times than once and...ah... what's that on your face?"

I wanted to giggle but held it back and huffed. "So often the same reaction. He told me you were a good mate. Surely you know about his fetish for a little feminine facial hair?"

"Ah..."

I winked. "He says it tickles him in all the right places."

Larry laughed as my over-acting hit home. "Oh, good. A piss-taker. That makes a change."

I kicked myself for asking but the words were out of my mouth before I engaged my brain. "From what?"

Larry took a hip flask from his pocket, unscrewed it and swigged. "From the normal posse of poseurs that have him in their sights. Designer-loving girls in search of a designer lifestyle, if you get my drift?"

I squirmed. "Ah…end of subject. I'm sure if Mark wants me to know that kind of stuff, he'll tell me himself."

Larry flicked me an airy wave of his hand. "Chill. I'm not sharing secrets. You hang around long enough and he won't have to tell you. You'll be tripping over one or another of them everywhere you go."

I snorted as a picture of me weaving through an obstacle course of raving beauties, each with their foot stuck out, tickled me. I smiled. "Fabulous. I'll look forward to it—but as of now, 'nuff said. Thanks."

Beth walked out of the sitting room, sat on the stair one above mine and looked over my shoulder. Larry grinned. "A family trait, is it?"

"Absolutely. You should see our nana's Foo Man Chu."

"Let alone my mum's Tom Selleck," Beth added.

I smiled at her and made the introductions. "Beth, meet Mark's mate, Larry. Larry, my cousin Beth. Larry's a little early to the après ski and has nicked Mark's phone."

Larry laughed. "I protest. I didn't nick it. He gave it to me."

"Misappropriated, then."

Larry's face disappeared to be replaced with a snowy mountainside, floodlights illuminating the path of the ski run as early evening darkness closed in. "So, there you go. Legitimate usage is restored."

I watched a blue speck become larger and larger, racing downward with increasing speed, then slow and stop as the incline flattened. Mark raised his goggles, unclipped his skis and walked closer.

"Why is my phone turned that way around? You said you wouldn't, but you have, haven't you?"

Larry hooted. "Of course I have, you sucker!"

"Give it here!"

I smiled as Mark's face steadied on the screen. Beth kissed her fingers in his direction then continued her progress up the stairs as I asked, "The schnapps is going down well, then?"

Mark gazed at me and my tummy flipped at the warmth I saw in his eyes. "Just a bit. He took a toss earlier so retired early from the runs to nurse his wounded pride."

Larry's voice answered, although I couldn't see his face. "Piss off! Like you wouldn't have been tucking into your own hip flask this time last year."

His voice receded as Mark moved away, his gaze not leaving my face. "But this time last year we weren't allowed to be an item and now we are. I'm not interested in partying with anyone but you."

I smiled into his eyes. "And me, you. While us being a couple wasn't possible, I could hide what I felt but now, I look back and wonder how I ever did."

"You'd give up your family Christmas to be here with me?"

"Like a shot."

"I love you, Ellie."

"I love you, too."

Mark smiled. "Have you no instructions for me with that, my little she-dragon?"

I puckered him a kiss. "So, go and celebrate with your boozy friend and I will go and play silly games. Then get into bed wanting me as I will get into bed wanting you."

"So much. I'm counting the days."

Beth trod down the stairs behind me. "Bloody hell! Are you two still at it?"

Mark laughed and I swatted her leg as she stepped past me. "Bugger off, mouth almighty!"

"Yeah, yeah. Hark who's talking...or should I say yelping!" she told him.

"Beth!"

She flicked her hip, shimmied her butt in my direction and walked into the sitting room.

Mark grinned. "Because?"

My cheeks heated. "We weren't the only ones in the guest rooms at the pub."

"Aaron?" he guessed.

I smiled. "Yeah. Beth's fancied him like crazy since she was in her teens but Aaron's six years older. Fifteen to twenty-one doesn't work but twenty-three to twenty-nine isn't such a stretch."

Aunt Mary's voice sounded through the open door. "Ellie, can you grab a damp cloth from the kitchen? Alma's missed her mouth with her spoon and has trifle down her front."

Mark laughed. "Speak later?"

"For sure." I blew him a kiss, cut the connection and returned to the sitting room with the means to mop off Alma. She departed at six-thirty and we played our Christmas games of charades, Guess Who? and team-relay tiddlywinks until midnight. I tottered off to bed quite a lot fuller of food and wine than I usually liked to be. Our Boxing Day was a re-run of Christmas, without the presents, and I woke on the twenty-seventh feeling absolutely stuffed to the gills, so took Scampi for a long walk. It helped a little, until the turkey reappeared in the form of a hearty stew at lunchtime and a savory pie at supper. Mark called every day, and by the time I went to bed on the twenty-eighth, much as I loved my family and my mum's home cooking, I felt more than ready to return to my flat.

The next morning, Dad drove me to the station in plenty of time to catch the ten-twenty to London and four hours later I dumped my travel bag in my living room then headed out to stock the larder.

I thought of the meals Mark had ordered at the hotel as I walked to the supermarket and visited the wet fish counter when I arrived. The fishmonger weighed and bagged sea bass fillets, then I added French beans to the basket and the ingredients for a chili butter. Milk and other essentials joined it, and by the time I added a bottle each of wine, gin and tonic, my basket had reached the limit of what I could carry, so I paid and staggered home.

My fridge looked satisfyingly full after I'd put my shopping inside it. I picked up my travel bag and took it upstairs to empty and repack for my stay at Mark's, opened my wardrobe and selected skinny jeans, knee-length boots with a square four-inch heel and a long-sleeved ribbed top with a cleavage-flattering V-cut neckline. Next, I added a plunge-front lace bodysuit that, teamed with my soft leather biker jacket, could be used to dress up the jeans if I needed to. Having no idea whether Mark had plans for us to go out on New Year's Eve, I selected two dresses, one short and more club-wear than the other, which was calf-length and made of soft jersey.

I looked at the pile on my bed, picked out underwear to go with each outfit then had an uncharacteristic fit of dithering and threw a thick sweater, leggings, a short skirt, black tights, two more tops, flat pumps and heeled courts onto the pile. I laughed when I surveyed the result but packed the lot anyway. I walked downstairs to pre-prepare the red chilis so I wouldn't have the burn of having done so on my fingers the next day. Mark messaged me when I sat on the sofa with a small salad for my supper, which was all my well-fed belly could manage after a week of stuffing myself with Christmas goodies.

I'm packed and checked in ready for 9am flight tomorrow. Can't wait to get home and see you. xx

And me you xx Tho – groan, groan – I need the footie run out after a week of Mum's dinners. You okay to eat in? I'll cook.

Great. Something light? I've had the exercise but the food here has been over-rich. I'm hoping not to encounter any more cheese-goo for quite some time!

I giggled at my phone.

Not overly fondue of it, are you?

Not fondue of it being brought to the table as a complimentary appetizer at every meal! We've taken to asking them not to do so. I think we may be arrested for a gross affront to the national dish if we don't leave the country soon.

Lol. Come home, Mr. Walker. Sea bass with chili butter waiting for you here.

With you as the appetizer?

My mouth watered at the thought of his mouth between my legs and the sweet taste of his cock in mine.

And you for dessert.

Mmmm…drooling, my little she-dragon. See you tomorrow xx

Mmmm…can't wait, my beautifully edible man. xx

I scraped the remainder of my salad into the bin and walked up to bed smiling.

Chapter Eight

I woke in the morning to a thrill of anticipation running through my belly, jumped into the shower and paid particular attention to de-fuzzing my legs and muff, mindful of the tiny, white shorts I would be wearing for the match. I dressed in leggings and a tee, changed my bed linen and cleaned the wet room. That done, I looked around the rest of my flat and found little else to do, with it being small and easy to keep clean, so sat on the sofa with a coffee and thought of Mark boarding his plane and having to forgo more champagne in order to be able to drive when he landed. I sipped, but the longer I sat, the more my legs twitched with a need for activity, so I downed my coffee, rinsed the mug in the sink and returned to my bedroom.

I kept my sportwear in a drawer of my under-bed storage. I pulled my padded goalie jersey, long socks and shin pads out then rummaged deeper until I found my short-shorts lurking at the bottom and dressed, shortening the over-long length of my jersey by way of twisting the excess material into a knot I tied at my waist. My sport holdall resided on my wardrobe floor and I checked that my goalie gloves were inside then added clean underwear and a sport towel. The time on my phone told me it was still a couple of hours before the match kicked off, but I threw on a trackie and headed out anyway to work the twitches out of my legs by jogging laps of the pitch.

I saw plenty of pre-match activity going on when I arrived at the club. The coals in the barbecue pit were smoking and the concessions for ice cream, popcorn and hot donuts had arrived. I walked into the changing room to find Lucy and Sarah already inside. Lucy looked up from lacing her boots. "Hey, you're early too. We came to see what was going on and have a warm-up. Did you have a good Christmas?"

I nodded, put my holdall on the bench and took my chance to mention Mark to her while there weren't too many other ears around. "I had a fantastic one, thanks. A guy I'm quite into asked me out. He'll be stopping by the match at some point."

She puffed out. "Phew. I'm glad you said. I've been dithering over if or when to tell you, but Jay's been seeing someone else this last month or so."

I smiled. "Good. I hope it works out for him. He's a great guy."

Lucy nodded and we jogged outside to run the perimeter of the pitch to her calls of "Jog, lunge, jog, star-jump…" More of the team tagged on behind us and I could feel the Christmas sloth peel away from me as I exercised. The crowd began to gather around the pitch, pints of beer in plastic glasses in their hands and the smell of frying onions in the air. Lucy nodded in the direction of our changing room and we ran toward it and stripped off our trackies when we were inside.

Lucy twerked her butt as we cheered. "Let's get 'em, girls."

We ran out onto the pitch to see the guys sporting wigs of tumbling curls, pom-poms and hairy legs beneath their ra-ra skirts. Mandy shook her matching pom-poms, jumped and began her chant, "Two, four, six, eight... Who do we appreciate?"

I walked to the goal and wriggled my butt as I loosened up by stretching toward the cross bar as the rest of the team performed a 'touching their toes' routine to several ribald shouts. The men's team shook their false bosoms and pom-poms at us in response and I laughed as Liam's skirt flipped up and showed his red satin panties. The match kicked off and I snorted as the guys' skirts lifted when they ran and showed they must have had a group outing to an Ann Summers shop.

We cheated alarmingly throughout the first half, knocking pom-poms from hands to pantomime performances of outrage while Mandy's cheerleading squad performed on the sideline. At half-time she laughed at me. "I'm pretty sure the blue buckets are heavier."

That was likely true until fifteen minutes before the end of the match, when my heart beat harder at the sight of Mark making his way through the crowd, dropping folding money into every pink bucket he came across.

The full-time whistle blew. I joined in on our team celebratory group hug for winning the match ten-two then walked toward his smile. I pressed close when I reached him, brushed his cheek with my lips and felt his, soft on my skin as he kissed me, holding me to him in the small of my back. "Mmmm...I'm liking those little shorts."

I moved my lips to his ear, my groin tingling with anticipation. "Shall I save my shower for when we get back to mine? You could come play in the water?" Mark's cock twitched against my belly as he breathed, "Yeah, please. Now, pack it in, Ms. McAllister, before I go caveman and smack your pretty little arse as I carry you off."

I giggled and took a step back. "Yeah, yeah. You'd have to put on a good turn of speed to catch me and accomplish that."

Mark offered me his hand. "Mmmm. Challenge accepted when there's not a crowd looking on."

I laughed and put my hand in his. "Did I just see you altering the odds in favor of the girls, Mr. Walker?"

He smiled. "Absolutely. I'm looking forward to seeing eleven Dame Ednas next year. What's the after-match form?"

I walked him toward the clubhouse "Drinks at the bar and lots of them, but if I show my face for one, we can exit stage left if you'd like."

He squeezed my hand. "Yes to that. Every time."

I smiled. "Give me five to throw my trackie on and I'll meet you at the bar."

I left Mark at the door to the clubhouse and ran to the changing room.

Sarah, wrapped in her towel, grinned at me as I walked in. "Bloody hell, Ellie. Where'd you pick him up from?"

I glossed over how we'd met. "Oh, one of those seminar conference things." I put my tracksuit on over my kit, changed my boots for trainers and picked up my holdall. "See you in the clubhouse." Several catcalls concerning my eagerness to depart followed me out.

The guys' team hadn't changed after the match and were mingling with the crowd around the bar as I walked into it. Liam, a pint in his hand, his Dolly Parton curls bouncing as he laughed, was standing beside Mandy, and I saw Mark's head a few places behind them. I bumped my butt on Liam's on my way past. "Nice panties, that man."

Mandy blushed. "He didn't borrow them from me."

Liam batted his false lashes in her direction. "No, but I might let you try them on later if you're lucky."

I shook my head at her. "Don't go there. There could be anything lurking behind those pretties."

She giggled. "I bloody well hope there is! Do you want a drink, Ellie?"

I looked past her shoulder and saw two gin and tonics standing on the bar. "I'm good, thanks. Mark got me one."

Liam swiveled his head as I said Mark's name. "I knew I recognized that guy from somewhere. I just couldn't place him dressed down. You'd best get a wriggle on. The ice is melting in your drink."

I walked toward Mark and he passed me my glass. "That's Liam from the Savoy under all that makeup?"

I sipped and coughed it out. "Yep, so now the score's two-one to me on the meet-the-ex-lovers front. Liam's another of mine. Fresher's year, for a couple of months until we decided we liked each other better as mates."

Mark snorted his disbelief. "*We* decided?"

I laughed. "Okay, *I* decided. I'm too bossy for him and he's too laidback to push against it, which drove me nuts."

He smiled. "I like bossy. Clingy has me sprinting for the far horizon double-quick time."

Sarah and Cheryl walked up to the bar. I smiled, introduced them and Mark bought them a drink. Three more of the team walked in through the door, freshly showered, their newly-dried hair bouncy and loose rather than up in a more normal post-match high-tail, and I couldn't help but note as they headed in our direction that none of them had found the need to change out of their Cheeky Girl shorts, although Vicki had rustled up a tight, white tee and Samantha, her makeup bag. I nudged Sarah's arm. She followed my gaze and grinned as they crowded around us.

"Hey, Ellie, well played."

"The guys look fantastic, don't they?"

"And this is…?"

I looked at three expressions gazing at Mark to mirror those worn by at least half my work colleagues every time he walked through the office. I kept my voice pleasant but dispensed with the welcoming smile I'd given Sarah and Cheryl. "My boyfriend, Mark."

"Hi, Mark," Vicki said, her voice soft with so much feminine saccharine as to give me the desire to snort and raise my eyes heavenward. "Have you and Ellie been seeing each other long?"

"Don't be silly, Vicki. They can't have been," Samantha tittered with a wide-eyed flutter of her lashes. "Ellie was dating Jay up until recently. Remember?"

"Long enough," Mark replied and slipped his arm around my waist.

I finished the last mouthful of my drink, put my glass beside his on the bar and smiled at Sarah and Cheryl as I picked up my sport bag. "I'll message you later." Then nodded at the other three. "I'll see you after the New Year. Have a good one."

Mark followed me to the door. I paused to introduce him to Liam and Mandy on our way through and he asked when it swung shut behind us, "Real mates versus teammates?"

I put my free hand in his and nodded. "Yeah. I see Sarah and Cheryl outside of the footie and Lucy, our team captain, who also happens to be Jay's sister, who incidentally, has also moved on and is dating someone else. Have you got an overnight bag in your car? There's limited parking at my flat but it's only about a fifteen-minute walk away, so your car would be best left here overnight."

Mark clicked his key fob as we walked through the car park and took his holdall out of the boot. We walked on, hand in hand, and I pointed out the neighborhood delights as we passed them—the best hot-chicken shop, the speediest dry cleaners, the craft café where the knitting bee gathered and drank coffee to the fast click-click of their needles.

Mark smiled. "What it is about any London suburb that there must be at least four hot-chicken shops and three dry-cleaning outlets on every main road?"

I nodded my agreement. "And churches, even if they've been converted to swanky apartments. Where was your place when you worked for Chase?"

"Penge."

"Ah...*Penge*. A little farther out then."

Mark laughed. "It was all I could afford at the time and it was more of a bedsit than a flat, but at London prices, it still fetched enough for me to buy a two-bed apartment near Worthing when I set up the company with enough capital residue to match the amount my grandfather had lent me. I wish I'd been able to keep it, though. It was valued at double the price I got for it the last time I checked, let alone the fact that I'm in town on business so often I would have saved enough on hotel bills to make it worth keeping as an overnight bolt hole if I hadn't needed to cash in its value."

I squeezed his hand. "Bummer! But at least you can stay over at mine now and not have to cough up for a hotel. I'll get a key cut for you when town resumes 'business as usual' after the New Year's holidays."

Mark's smile lit his face. "You will?"

I laughed at his reaction. "Sure. Why wouldn't I?"

His cheek bones tinted a little pink. "Embarrassingly sad but true. Most of the interest I attract nowadays is from girls whose notion of sharing only works one way, me to them."

What Larry had said to me on our FaceTime chat came to mind. "Since Walker and Timpson became publicly profitable?"

Mark's color deepened a little more. "If it doesn't sound too cringingly up my own arse, I won't say I ever went halfway short of a date before I formed the company, but since it started showing a healthy profit, I've had my fingers burned more than once by a girlfriend with her own agenda. It took me a while to catch on. The possibility of anyone wanting to be with me for anything other than… ah…the pleasure of my company had never so much as entered my head."

It wasn't a far stretch to hazard a guess. "Laura? Did you suspect she was 'accidentally on purpose' trying to get pregnant to step your relationship up to the next level?"

Mark wrinkled his nose. "Yeah. I hated myself for thinking that way, but that was my suspicion. We'd talked about our hopes for an 'if and when' future but I don't think she wanted to wait. But before Laura, there was Katrina, who I finally realized could have taught masterclasses in manipulative sulking if not taken shopping in Oxford Street on the weekend, and after Laura, Sasha, who I'd been seeing for a few months until we went to a black-tie do like the one at the Savoy, where she spent the evening charming the socks off a bloke with more noughts on the end of his bank balance than mine. They're married now. She's thirty-one. He's seventy-nine."

I laughed at that one. "What a cow! Well, you're welcome to share my London space but I'll warn you now…magnificent it is not."

Mark smiled and put his arm around my waist. "It's everything." I put my free hand in the back pocket of his jeans and we walked on until we arrived at my apartment block.

I told Mark the code as I tapped on the security pad and let us in through the street door then dropped my sport bag to the floor and wound my arms around his neck when the doors to the tiny four-person elevator closed. We broke apart as it juddered to a stop then I led him to the door of my flat. I opened it and dropped my sport bag inside. Mark put his holdall alongside mine, looked around the space in front of him then upward to the waist-high glass and chrome screen of the open-plan mezzanine level. "Neat design." I pushed the front door shut behind us. "I like it. I viewed other new-builds with a more traditional bedroom space and they felt pokey to me compared to this one."

Mark walked to the floor-to-ceiling window with its view of the street and the unceasing line of traffic snaking along the road below. "This is a good feature. It lets in loads of natural light. It's what I looked for when I relocated from Worthing to Brighton."

"And did you get it?"

He turned, smiled and teased. "I may have. You'll find out tomorrow."

I eyed him up and down. "The Royal Pavilion hasn't been up for sale in recent times, has it?"

He laughed. "I'd run a mile if it ever was. If there's a building that would give me a permanent migraine to live in, it's that one." I smiled and didn't probe further, to save the reaction I sensed he was looking forward to from me when I saw his apartment in the morning.

I unlaced my trainers and took them to the slotted shoe storage under the coat rack. Mark did the same and hung his jacket on a spare hook. I took off my trackie top, shimmied out of its bottom half, removing my socks as I did so, then wiggled my butt cheeks in my Cheeky Girl shorts and looked at his stiffening crotch. "Shower time?"

I led the way up the stairs, switched on the shower in the wet room and turned to face Mark, who was standing in the doorway. He gazed as I unlatched my sport bra, took it off, along with my footie top, and dropped them both to the floor. He unfastened his shirt, then the zip of his jeans. I walked under the spray and the material became translucent, clinging to the lips and split of my mound.

His eyes gleamed his want as he freed his erection and I breathed deeper at the sight of his hard cock then unfastened the side zip of my shorts and shimmied out of them.

He stripped off the remainder of his clothes. I gazed at his muscled body as he walked closer and licked my lips. Wet with need, I turned and presented him with my rear view as I grasped the shower pole and bent forward at an angle to allow him to enter me from behind. With a soft growl, he pressed close, parted my pussy with his fingers and thrust in his cock. I mewled my appreciation as he found my breasts, squeezing on their fullness. His breath rasped as he slammed into me harder and faster. The hot water pouring down caressed my sensitized skin and I panted then pushed back against him until his greedy frenzy tipped me over the edge and I shouted as the waves of my climax spread through my pelvis.

"Mark... Fuck! Yes!"

He tensed, his thrusts shortening to his groan. "Oh, God. Sweetheart..."

We stilled, breathing hard. Mark eased out of me and held me to him as I straightened. I leaned against him and the hot water poured over us both until my heart rate slowed and I reached for the sponge and pumped squirts of shower gel onto it. He took it from me and circled it over my shoulders, down my back and over my butt. I turned as the suds ran down my legs and he squeezed more foam over my breasts and belly. Then I took the sponge from him, squirted more gel onto it and returned the favor, enjoying the feel of the muscled contours of his body.

I squeezed the last bubbling suds over my head when he was lathered, dropped the sponge, wound my arms around his neck and kissed him as the spray rinsed the soap from our bodies. I stepped back and turned off the water. "I'll get us some towels."

I took three from the hamper that stood between the wash basin and the frosted glass privacy door of the loo, out of reach of the shower spray, wrapped one around my hair, another around my body and gave Mark the third. He toweled off then tucked it around his waist.

"I'll bring up the bags," he offered.

I rubbed down and rough-dried my hair while he was gone then pulled on a pair of leggings and a vest-top. He unzipped his holdall and took out a toiletry bag when he returned. "I have more supplies at home. I could leave this here?"

I heard what he was really asking and smiled. "I'd like that."

He moved closer and kissed my hair. "And bring some things with you to leave at mine tomorrow?"

I looked at my bulging travel bag, pulled his face closer and kissed his lips. "Yep."

Mark took his toiletries to the wet room then pulled a pair of knee-length soft shorts and a tee from his bag and dressed. I took my phone from mine, decided anyone who wanted to speak to me tonight could wait until the morning, so put it beside the bed. I dropped my footie kit into my dirty washing basket and looked at Mark's discarded clothes.

"Does any of that need to go through the machine?"

His eyes gleamed his liking of my offer and he added his underwear and shirt to the hamper, transferred his phone from his jeans to his shorts pocket and followed me down to the kitchen.

I picked up my trackie on my way through the living room and whisked it out of sight behind the washer door. Mark looked around the small galley-style space.

"What can I do?"

I opened a cupboard and passed him a crusty bread baton and the butter dish then took the electric steamer out of another. "If you work the fridge end, I'll work the other. Booze, mixers and wine are chilling. Rummage for anything else you need. You have a choice of three drawers and four cupboards, so it won't be far." He opened the refrigerator door and reached for the wine. I moved behind him, snagged the bass fillets and green beans from under his arm and took two steps sideways to the sink. He found the corkscrew and glasses, opened the wine and poured as I set the timer on the steamer and began to heat the skillet. He passed me a glass then hunted down the bread board and knife. "Where are we eating?"

"Given the space available, I had to choose between a table or a desk. The desk won, so on a lap tray sitting on the sofa."

He smiled, took the wine bottle through to the living room and set it on the coffee table. I looked at the time display on the oven clock and called after him. "Flick the telly on? The quarter and semis of the World Darts are just starting on Sky Sport One. The channel's pre-programmed on my favorites list."

The low hum of a large, boozy crowd sounded, then, "I love you even more now."

"Oh, yeah. Why's that?"

Mark smiled as he walked into the kitchen. "Because you don't have a single soap, reality show or shopping channel on your viewing selection."

I puckered him an air-kiss and flipped the bass fillets. "Nope. Sports, comedy and music, in that order."

"About the same as mine, although with the addition of the Lifestyle channel, as I have a secret addiction to MasterChef in all its many varieties."

"Why? Thinking of applying?"

Mark laughed. "No way. I can't cook to speak of, apart from the basics, but there's just something about the show that pulls me in."

I flipped the fish onto warmed plates, spooned burned brown chili butter over them and added the beans.

He sniffed in the aroma. "But perhaps *you* should. That smells really good."

I looked at the bread board. "And you've just lost the team challenge. Jump to it, man. That baton is not going to cut and butter itself."

He grinned and did so. "Yes, my little she-dragon." I took the lap trays from the cupboard, added cutlery, our wine glasses then our plates as he finished with the knife and placed slices of buttered bread beside the fish.

I picked up my tray and Mark followed me through to the living room. We sat on the sofa to a cry of *'one-hundred-and-eighty'* from the television and ate, drank wine and mopped up chili butter with our bread as we watched the match. Full after we'd finished, I stacked the trays, took them to the kitchen then ignored them to deal with later and poured two gin and tonics. He took his from me, stretched out his legs, put his feet up on the coffee table and offered me his arm. I relaxed against him beneath it and tucked my legs up beside me as he kissed my shoulder.

"That was lovely. Thank you."

I sipped my drink and smiled. "I'm glad you enjoyed it. Your turn tomorrow."

"Brighton can be a bit hit or miss on New Year's Eve if you haven't pre-booked, so I thought a late, leisurely lunch then back to mine for fizz and fireworks. There's a pretty spectacular display on the waters just off the beach during the evening and my apartment is frontline."

I snuggled in tighter. "Perfect."

He tightened his arm around me. "Yeah…"

His phone began to chirp. I sat straighter, so he could reach into his pocket, and he swore softly when he looked at the screen then let it ring out without answering.

"It's Angel. She keeps calling even though I've asked her not to."

I breathed in deep, squished the green-eyed monster as it tried to raise its head and made myself ask, "Oh, dear… What does she want?"

Mark put his phone on the coffee table and shrugged. "Nothing in particular. That's what's odd. Angel's got a busy social life. She breezes in and out of town. She never just calls to ask, *'Hi, how are you doing?'*"

His answer soothed my fear that I was about to discover more detail of his relationship with Angel than I would be comfortable to know, so I relaxed and snuggled back under his arm.

"You told her about us?"

He nodded. "Yeah. I saw her home to her place after she turned up in the wine bar. She passed out on the sofa, so I hung around until she came to in case she vom'd and met her for a coffee once she'd sobered up the day after. She was a bit sheepish about the state she'd been in, but we chatted. I said my bit and she was cool about it, wished me all the best and dashed off to get ready for a party she was going to that evening. Then a couple of days later she phoned, and it was as if our conversation over coffee hadn't happened and that's how it has gone on…like *Groundhog Day*. I stopped taking her calls while I was skiing. There's no point. I'll have to sort this in person."

I sipped my drink as a picture built. "So, she's very pretty and very popular. Has she ever been told 'thanks but no thanks'?"

Mark tightened his arm around me. "I don't know, sweetheart. We weren't that involved in each other's lives, which suited me. I saw Angel now and then, depending on what she was up to, because the woman I wanted to be with wasn't free and I wasn't sure you ever would be. You think she's having trouble accepting what I'm saying because no guy has ever called 'time' on her before?"

"Maybe. And maybe more so if you named me. She was less than impressed at the wine bar. I know she was squiffy, but if she remembers me, being sober won't alter that opinion."

Mark winced. "Damn! I'd hoped you were out of earshot when she spouted off."

I smiled. "That she broadcast her opinion loud enough for the whole bar to hear was out of order, but it was my choice to project that particular image. Her summing up of me is what I'd aimed for, if a little noisy."

Mark kissed on the top of my head. "I'll straighten things out next week."

I put my glass down on the coffee table and tilted my face for a kiss. He put his drink alongside mine and pulled me into his arms. I slid my hand inside his tee as our tongues entwined, explored the muscled contours of his chest then stroked my fingertips toward his happy trail. He tugged on the back of my top. I took it off and dropped it to the floor. He gazed at the fullness of my breasts, standing proud with nipples erect, and my pussy wettened at the gleam in his eyes as I gazed back my appreciation of the beauty of his upper body.

He urged me backward, lay over me and rubbed his hard chest against my softer one.

"Time for some messy play?" he asked.

I looked into his eyes. "Oh, yeah?"

He pinned my arms above my head and nibbled my bottom lip. "Don't move. Back in a minute."

I held my position as he walked up the stairs then returned with a slim, white gift box. He placed it on the coffee table, peeled off his shorts and stood before me, his cock ready for action. I breathed harder as he tugged off my leggings, dropped them to the floor then opened the box and took out my Christmas gift to him. He placed it on my pubic mound, lay over me, pressed his groin to mine and grasped my hands. "Now we wait for it to melt and see who can smear it the farthest."

I giggled and the rigid shape between us softened. I writhed beneath him to move the slick up the length of his cock, realized when I did so that it placed my tummy button in the direct line of fire and squealed. "Mark!"

He ground his hips against mine and the melted chocolate slivered into the split of my pussy. "Yes, sweetheart?"

I squirmed to no avail as he pinned my hands, swirled his pelvis and pushed soft chocolate into all the hidden creases between my legs until I squeaked. "You worked this out in advance."

He kissed my lips. "I never said I was going to play fair."

I moved my head and bit his shoulder.

He tensed. "Ellie, yes."

I fastened my mouth on his neck and sucked.

He breathed deeper and continued to move against me until I kissed the bite mark I'd left on his skin. He freed my hands, took his weight on his knees then licked his lips as he looked downward at the result. "Mmmm. Time for dessert, I think."

I followed his eyes and saw the majority of the soft chocolate molded in and around my pussy, so parted my legs and gave myself up to the pleasure of his mouth nibbling, licking and sucking every crease. I moaned as his tongue circled my clit. He slipped one finger and another through my wetness then inside me and my back arched as I gasped.

"Let me taste you too?" I asked.

He straddled my chest and offered his cockhead to my mouth. I took it in, sweet with an added dash of bitter chocolate, and sucked. His voice caught in the back of his throat when I increased the vacuum of my mouth and stroked up and down his shaft. I kept up the rhythm until he groaned and pulled away.

"I need to be in you."

I looked into his eyes. "Yes, now…"

He held my gaze, lowered his body, parted my wet lips and plunged his shaft inside. I gasped as he filled me. "Oh, so good!"

He growled and thrust—hard, fast and urgent. I met him, hip to hip, wrapped my legs around his thighs and dug my fingertips into his taut butt cheeks. He pounded harder and my climax mounted. I lifted my hand and slapped.

He groaned. "Yes…" His thrusts shortened as I slapped again and again and again, and my climax raced free when he stiffened in the throes of his orgasm and called my name.

"Oh, God! Oh, fuck! Ellie... Ellie...."

Aftershocks spread through my belly as we stilled and I mewled with the pleasure of them. Mark withdrew and turned to his side. I curled against him, my head nestled on his shoulder, and, breathing hard, we lay wrapped in each other's arms until, satiated, my eyelids fluttered closed.

He stroked down my back. "Bed?"

I untangled my limbs from his and put my feet to the floor. "Yeah." I turned off the television. We picked up our clothes and took them upstairs, then we used the bathroom and washed away the last smears of chocolate. I checked my phone was within reach on the bedside table and snuggled under Mark's arm.

I woke in the morning ahead of my alarm, swallowed my pill and spooned into his side for another hour until he stirred, turned and snuggled his face into my breasts. My nipples hardened as his stiffening cock dug against my thigh and I smiled.

"Mr. Walker, are you wanting something from me?"

He stroked through my early morning arousal. "I think I might be."

I parted my legs for him to move his fingers, sighed as he probed my wet center and reached for his shaft. His breathing deepened as I moved my hand up and down his erection with a soft squeeze while I traced the fingers of my other hand over and around his balls until he moaned. "Ellie..."

I released him and parted my legs. He lay over me, eased his cockhead in and asked for my mouth with his. I kissed him deeply as he moved his shaft in, slowly, inch by inch, then undulated his hips against mine.

"So beautifully wet, sweetheart. You ready for me?"

I writhed beneath him. "Please…and hard." His first thrust speared me. "Oh, fuck! That's good…"

He sank his teeth into my neck and crashed against me fast and hard.

I pumped my hips to meet his, panting, and I pushed his hand to my breast. He grasped the fullness of it, squeezed and I yelled the joy of my climax as it spread through my belly and thighs. "Fuck! Yes!"

Mark groaned as he let go. "Yes, sweetheart…"

I turned into his arms after he withdrew and we lay drowsing for a while until a certain need caught me. I kissed his lips. "Loo." He unwrapped his arms and I grabbed my wrap on my way to the wet room.

I called through the door after I flushed. "Do you want to shower while I put the coffee on? Unless you'd prefer tea to go with a bacon sandwich?"

"I'll go with coffee and bacon, thanks."

I swapped places with him, folded the duvet back on itself to allow the bed to air and walked downstairs. Mark joined me, smelling gorgeous, as the bacon sizzled in the pan. He sniffed. "Heaven."

I smiled and nodded toward the coffee pot. "It's just about done if you want to pour." He did so and I placed hot bacon between slices of buttered bread, then we took our breakfast through to the living room. I flicked the telly on and tuned into the local news station in time to hear the presenter detailing the many security arrangements and traffic restrictions being put in place around the capital for the safety of the crowds expected for New Year's Eve celebrations later.

Mark swallowed a mouthful of his sandwich. "The sooner we're out of the city, the better, I think. I'll deal with the dishes while you shower?"

I nodded, finished the last of my coffee and left him to it as I ran up the stairs then showered and dressed in double-quick time. I plaited my towel-dried, damp hair into a French pleat, and, after cleaning my teeth, used a quick squirt of perfume and I was ready.

Mark came out of the kitchen as I walked down the stairs with my travel bag in my hand. "Blimey, that was speedy for a…a…"

I laughed at his hesitation. "For a girl?"

He smiled. "Yep."

I blew him a kiss. "I'll glam up for lunch at your place. Grab your holdall and let's get out of here."

I closed the front door behind us. We walked to the football club and found it empty of life when we arrived to a sprinkling of cars in the grounds that had been abandoned overnight like Mark's. He stowed our bags on the narrow bench seat at the back of the cabin and I climbed into the passenger side, very happy to be going with him rather than watching him drive off without me. He started the engine, nosed into the traffic and we departed the capital at an even worse speed than its usual stop-start snail's pace.

Chapter Nine

Mark put his foot down as we hit the motorway an hour later and we drove along the Brighton seafront, past his office then the marina, another hour after that. He turned into a car park adjacent to a red-brick apartment block standing four floors higher than its bow-windowed Regency neighbors, parked and cut the engine. "This is as close as we get. Parking in central Brighton is nearly as impossible as in London."

I looked out of the side window. "What was the building originally?"

"A luxury hotel built to compete with The Grand, but The Grand won that battle, so it was converted into apartments during the eighties. I bought mine when the block was refurbished about four years ago."

I climbed out of the car and noticed a modern glass structure on the roof-line. "What's that they've built on the top? An observation deck or something?"

Mark looked into my eyes and winked.

I laughed as I got it. "That's your apartment, isn't it?"

He smiled. "Yep. I bought it for the views out over the sea."

He took our bags from the bench seat, opened the boot and lifted out his larger holiday suitcase then locked the car and led the way. Pulling our wheeled luggage, we crossed the road and walked to the large, canopied double-doors of the entrance. They swished open on our approach. I looked around at what must have been a fabulous hotel lobby in its day as I followed him in and saw an ornately carved plasterwork ceiling supported by thick, marble pillars. Running the length of one side stood a high-sheen mahogany check-in desk now replaced with an array of post boxes, each with its own numeric key pad.

Mark pressed the call button for one of two lifts and pressed 'seven' when the door closed behind us. There was a choice of only one front door when the elevator doors opened. Mark unlocked it and stepped inside. "There's only my study, a coat cupboard and the stairs up to the rest of the apartment on this floor." I walked into a space larger than the whole of my flat and laughed. "I'm surprised you didn't get an attack of claustrophobia staying at mine."

He smiled. "Apart from the access to the sea, it's the other reason why I opened a business in Brighton and didn't stay in London when I left Chase."

I took off my coat and he hung it in the cupboard with his. "I'll bring the bags up later." He took my hand. We walked up two flights of polished wooden stairs and I blinked at the brightness as I walked into a huge modern living space with floor-to-ceiling bi-fold doors on three sides that opened onto a wrap-around deck, the furnishings of white and cream in the room standing on a floor of cherry-walnut. I stepped closer to the glass and looked out at the sea, sparkling blue in the winter sun, no more than a hundred yards distant.

"Wow. It's a beautiful spot."

Mark stood behind me, draped his arms over my shoulders and kissed my neck. "You'd be happy to spend time here?"

I leaned back against him. "Oh, I think I could get used to it."

He squeezed his arms around me. "Depending on work commitments, we could share our time between our two flats?"

I smiled. "Sounds like a plan."

He offered me his hand. "Come and see the rest of it."

I put my hand in his and looked at the open-plan kitchen at the back of the room, glistening with white, glossy units and fittings of sparkling chrome, then at two bedrooms of pristine paleness, each with a gleaming en suite bathroom. "It's gorgeous, but how do you manage to keep it in this state? It must take hours to clean."

Mark smiled. "Yeah, it does — but not by me. I have the Molly Maid service in three times a week — Monday, Wednesday and Friday, except bank holidays."

"Thank the Lord for that," I said. "I don't mind doing my turn but, blimey, this place is high-maintenance."

He laughed. "Well, on that subject, I left a shopping list, so let's go and check the fridge and I'll make some coffee."

Mark opened the fridge and I looked inside to see it fully stocked with just about everything from bacon and eggs through to olives and charcuterie from the deli. "Is there anything in there you want to eat?" he asked.

Cassie O'Brien

I spotted pastries in a see-through plastic cake box. "Nothing much if we're doing lunch. Perhaps a Danish to go with the coffee?"

He handed them to me and nodded toward a cupboard. "The plates are there, the cutlery in the drawer beneath it."

I set out the pastries while Mark brewed the coffee and we sat on either side of the breakfast bar. He phoned the restaurant, spoke to someone called Philippe and reserved a table for two o'clock while I poured the coffee and asked, "It's somewhere you eat at regularly?"

He nodded. "Yeah. Brighton, for a city, is also quite villagey. People tend to have their favorite haunts and other venues they avoid like the plague. I have three or four restaurants I really like, but if I just want a drink, I'll go to the sailing club rather than a bar."

I looked at the glass-topped dining table sitting on a cream marble base with seating for eight. "And dinner parties?"

He shrugged. "Not so much these last three years. I haven't been half of a couple as such since I split with Laura, so the table only gets used if I've got family staying over."

"Mum and Dad will be able to stay with me when I upsize. My place is so small and open-plan, they book into the local hotel when they come south."

"Do they visit often?"

I shook my head. "Only once or twice a year — to take in a show, normally. What about your parents?"

"About the same. They're only half an hour down the road, so it's mainly when there's something on that includes a drink or several and they don't want to drive."

I finished my coffee and set down the cup. Mark ate the last of his pastry. I stacked the plates and took them to the sink.

He stood. "I'll bring the bags up."

I washed the dishes while he was gone then joined him in the master bedroom after he wheeled his suitcase through. The side wall was of mirrored doors and he slid one open and I saw hanging rails and shelf space containing nothing. "There's plenty of space. My gear doesn't even take up half of it."

The contents of my travel bag disappeared into a small corner when I unpacked. I picked out my plunge-front lace bodysuit to dress up my skinny jeans with my soft leather biker jacket to make it lunchtime suitable. I used the en suite loo first. Mark followed after me. He was changed and ready while I was still giving my face the full works for New Year's Eve. He left me to it in favor of loading his laptop and checking his emails, and once I was satisfied with my makeup, I extended the length of my legs by way of knee-high boots with their four-inch heels.

Mark's eyes gleamed his appreciation when I sauntered into the living room and I gave him mine as I gazed at the fit of his black jeans topped with a pale linen shirt and tailored jacket. My phone in my jacket pocket and my payment cards in the back of my jeans dispensed with any need to carry a bag, and I followed him down the stairs and through the soft swish of the street door into air that was crisp but not so cold as to make a heavier coat a necessity. I put my hand in his and we strolled along the seafront toward The Lanes until we reached a small French bistro.

The maître d' smiled as we entered and he greeted Mark by name. Mark enquired if he'd had a good

Christmas while we walked to a table in the bow-fronted window with a view onto the bustle of The Lanes. A waiter brought menus to us.

I opened mine, saw it had no prices listed so closed it and offered it back with a polite smile. "I'll take a regular menu, thanks."

The waiter acknowledged my request with a nod, whisked it away, returned with another then left us to decide on our order.

I opened mine and explained. "I've disliked guest menus since I was invited out for dinner and discovered sometime later that the truffle in the risotto I'd ordered was a specialty and priced at about twenty quid a shaving. I was mortified to have added so much to the guy's bill."

Mark nodded his agreement. "I would have been too. I hate being mugged off, and regardless of how successful my company is or becomes, I always will."

Philippe the maître d' reappeared with two small pottery cups of pear cider and a dish of olives for an aperitif, placed them on the table then turned toward the street door as it opened. Mark glanced at it and a look passed between them as two slim and attractive women walked in. Philippe hurried away.

"Ladies, how lovely to see you again. How you do enjoy our menu. That's every day this week you've eaten with us."

I took stock of the new arrivals as the brunette, her hair precision-cut into a sleek bob, wearing Gucci accessories that looked the real thing, answered, "Yes, your chef is a wonder. I see the window table is taken but the one behind it is free?"

"Unfortunately, it's reserved. Such a busy time of year. Although I do have a table available toward the back of the bistro, if you would like it?"

The brunette's friend, her long, black hair glossily straightened to within an inch of its life, adjusted this year's must-have tote from Michael Kors over her arm and drawled, "It will have to do, I suppose."

I watched as they walked through the bistro behind Philippe, their gazes sweeping past me as if I was the invisible woman while keeping Mark in their eyeline. He kept his fixed on the wine list until, with a waft of Chanel, they were past us. I bit my lip to stifle my urge to laugh as he raised his eyes and looked at my face with a small tut.

"Something tickling your funny bone is there, Ms. McAllister?"

A small giggle escaped me as I nodded. "Who are they? Do you know them?"

He shook his head. "Not in the slightest. Of the restaurants I like, this is my favorite and they started turning up about a month ago."

I thought of my obstacle course of raving beauties and giggled again. "You get followed around the place like this a lot, do you?"

Mark smiled with a shrug. "Enough to know there's nothing I can do about it. I'm in a public space. But if they get no reaction from me, they'll give up and vamoose after a while. Have you decided on your order? Do you want red or white?"

I returned his smile then sipped my cider. "I'd like the lobster bisque followed by the dressed crab salad, thank you."

Mark looked at his menu then placed our order. "White again, then. I'll have the scallops and the bouillabaisse."

The waiter brought the wine to the table, poured and our first course arrived shortly after. I breathed in a wonderful, savory aroma. "Oh, this smells good."

Mark smiled and cut into his scallop.

I dipped my spoon into my bowl and the brunette woman strolled past our table with her phone to her ear.

"Yes, sweetie. I'll just pop outside so I can hear you properly."

Halfway down my bowl she returned, trying to make eye contact with Mark as she made her way back through the restaurant to no avail as he concentrated on his scallops. She reappeared again as our first-course plates were being cleared, heading toward the Ladies, girl-flirting with her dark-haired friend loudly enough to attract attention.

I sipped my wine and, as the waiter set our main courses on the table, the women exited the toilets and 'darling'd' each other all the way back to their table. Mark and I carried on with our meal and he told me more about his holiday to two more passes through the restaurant by the two of them, and, as I laid down my cutlery, the brunette swayed past us to take yet another phone call outside. I caught Mark's eye and couldn't resist letting go of the laughter I'd been choking back for over an hour.

He huffed. "Ellie McAllister, you are a very wicked woman. You could be helping me out with this, you know."

I looked at him and saw, not a twinkle in his eyes, but the quiet stillness I associated with his dealing with more serious matters during working hours.

"You think? How's that?"

He reached into his pocket, took out a small square box and my heart gave an almighty thump against my ribs as I recognized the name inscribed in silver lettering on the top of it as one of the retail outlets at his resort. He gazed into my eyes and opened it.

"Take me off the market?"

I looked at a sparkling, brilliant-cut solitaire standing proud of a gold band and smiled to the delighted dance of my innards. "Yep."

Mark's grin lit his face. "Finger."

I held out my left hand. He plucked the ring from its velvet bed, slid it on and it fit. "It's very beautiful. Thank you. A good guess or…?"

He smiled. "Or I might have noticed when I was holding the ice pack on your hand that my pinky finger is about the same size as your ring finger."

I smiled back at him. "Very sneaky, Mr. Walker."

He took my hand to his mouth, kissed my fingers and mouthed, *'I love you.'*

I whispered softly under my breath, "I love you, too."

Philippe bounced up to our table and it became apparent that his sharp eyes had missed nothing of Mark's proposal or my acceptance as he asked, "That is a ring? She has said yes? Congratulations are in order?"

Mark nodded. Philippe waved his arms in the direction of two waiters then clapped his hands. "Release the corks. A glass of champagne for everyone on the house. We have a wonderful event to celebrate."

The waiters loaded trays with bubbling wine and offered the flutes to the other guests in the restaurant.

The brunette and her friend paid their bill and left without taking one. Mark and I sipped and acknowledged the toasts ringing around the room until I laid my glass down, empty.

"Can we go home now? I should Skype Mum and Dad."

He smiled. "And maybe Beth, then Larry?"

I laughed. "That should be a hoot. What about your peeps?"

He pushed his chair back and stood. "I told my mum what I hoped when I bought the ring. They're flying back overnight. Come and meet them next weekend?"

"Sure. I can't wait to do so."

Mark settled the bill on our way out. I opened the street door to a darkened sky and the glitter of holiday lights and spotted a jewelry shop up ahead. "Okay, you. Get in there. It's no use me taking you off the market unless the market knows I have."

Mark smiled. I tugged on his hand and pushed open the shop door. The sales assistant stepped forward and showed us what he had available and the choice came down to one of two—a gold band engraved with a Celtic design or a platinum band inset with a small diamond.

Mark looked at me. "You pick. I chose for you."

I selected the platinum band. Mark reached for his wallet. I whipped out my debit card from the pocket of my jeans and handed it over.

"Uh-uh. No way are you paying for your own engagement ring. You bought mine. I'm buying yours." The payment processed and I slid Mark's ring onto his finger while the sales assistant dropped the empty box into a small carrier bag with the receipt. We left the shop and stopped in a shadowed, darkened doorway for the kiss we couldn't have in the restaurant then walked on, hip to hip, with an arm around each other's waists. The lobby door swished open as we arrived at it. We walked in and Mark looked at the ex-check-in desk.

"Perhaps I'd best grab my post."

I stopped walking beside one of the thick supporting pillars to give him space to open his mailbox. "Sure. I'll hang on here while you get it."

He nodded, walked to the side wall of numbered boxes and reached out for the pin entry pad. I took a pace behind the pillar so as not to oversee the code as he did, heard the electronic beep of two numbers being entered then the soft swish of the lobby doors and Angel's voice.

"Hey, you're home! I thought I'd swing by and see if you were about. Was the phone signal dreadful in the Alps? I called several times while you were there and again last night."

Then Mark's.

"Angel, what are you doing here?"

"Oh, well, it's been a couple of weeks since our little tiff, so I thought—"

Mark cut her off. "Stop, please. I made my position quite clear before I went skiing. Ellie and I are together now and I've asked you several times to stop calling me."

She answered with a low laugh. "Oh, bloody hell, Mark! Not geek-girl from the wine bar? If you want me to take you seriously, at least name someone that provides a little more competition to me than her. I know it was naughty of me to turn up at your work tiddled, but surely you've forgiven me by now?"

I decided I'd heard enough, unzipped my biker jacket and parted it to make obvious what my work attire normally concealed then walked over to them, stood beside Mark and stared her down. "Although, maybe some of us just prefer to keep our personal assets to ourselves during business hours."

She had the grace to blush as she stared back at me and made the connection. I threaded my arm through Mark's and her eyes darted to the diamond sparkling on my finger, then toward his ring as he laid his hand on mine. The color staining her cheeks deepened and she looked at Mark.

"Well, if you'd just shown me a pic, I would have got the message."

I squeezed a little pressure onto his arm and answered her. "No. Mark told you his choice and his decision, and you should have respected that even if, in your opinion, I look like the back end of a bus." I nodded over her shoulder in the direction of the lobby doors. "The exit's behind you. *Use it.*"

"Oh, bloody charming!" she shot back at me but turned on her heel and did so.

I watched the doors close behind her. "You still need to get your post."

Mark smiled. "Nah, it can wait. Let's get upstairs before we get waylaid by anyone else tonight."

I unthreaded my arm and put my hand in his. "Okay. Let's go and get some fizz."

We walked to the lift and he pushed the call button. I stepped inside to thoughts the quantity of space available upstairs and wound my arms around his neck while inventing the only type of rules I hoped to need in the future as a game of 'strip-me-naked-hide-and-seek' floated into my mind while the elevator moved upward.

Want to see more from this author?
Here's a taster for you to enjoy!

The Girls' Club
Cassie O'Brien

Excerpt

The moon hid behind the trees to leave the path a dark trip hazard of exposed, misshapen tree roots for us to find. I grabbed Jules' hand to steady myself and giggled into the warm night air as I stumbled. Jules giggled beside me.

"Shouldn't 'ave had the last one, Ness."

"The B-52 or the pinta piña colada?"

Jules lurched against me as her shoe snagged and caught. I laughed and pushed her upright again.

"Both. Should'a got a taxi, though."

"Only gotta get through the par – "

Jules' chin hit her chest and her knees crumpled as the back of my head exploded with pain from a curled fist that I glimpsed out of the corner of my eye as my legs gave way. My butt hit the path and I joined my scream to Jules', kicked out with my foot and caught the thigh of the chunky male closing the gap between us with the high heel of my shoe.

"Fuck! You bitch!"

The man made a grab for my ankle. I brought my other leg up, kicked, caught his thigh again with the heel of my other shoe and screamed louder. Jules' shrill cry cut off with a crack of bone on bone.

"What the fuck you doin', man?"

"She's kicking me."

"Just shut 'er the fuck up!"

The man lurched forward and dropped his weight onto my legs, used it to stifle my struggles and cut off my voice with a hand clamped over my mouth and nose as I writhed beneath him. I fought for breath, aimed desperate fingernails at brown eyes beneath a knitted hat pulled down low and flashes of light swam before my eyes as a clenched hand connected with the side of my head.

"Get the fuck on with it! I've got the other one's jewelry and bag."

My arm was forced to my side and a heavy-heeled boot crunched down. My fingers were bent and twisted as my grandmother's eternity ring was yanked from my finger, my attempted high-pitched howl silent without air to give it sound. The chain of my necklace bit into my neck before it snapped. The flesh of my stomach caught fire as my belly bar was ripped from it without being undone. I curled into a fetal ball as feet ran away. I sucked air into my lungs in desperate gulps and my stomach heaved.

My butt hit the floor again and I woke, covered in sweat. I ran to my bathroom just in time to kneel and vomit into the toilet bowl. I kneeled straighter after my stomach emptied and my bedroom lit up over my shoulder.

"Ness? Another? So soon?" Jules asked from the bathroom door.

I nodded and flushed.

"I'll get you a water."

I ran the cold tap in the sink while Jules was gone, splashed my face and cleaned my teeth. Jules walked into my bedroom and handed me a bottle of mineral water as I straightened the duvet on top of my bed. I took the bottle and sat, legs out, my back against the headboard. Jules leaned back alongside me.

"So, walk me through your day."

I sighed and closed my eyes. Jules squeezed my hand.

"I know it sometimes seems pointless, babe, but it's got to be done. I'm sure there must be something that reminds you of the mugging and triggers a memory in your subconscious to make you dream about it, even if you don't recognize that something for what it is at the time."

I opened my eyes and drank a mouthful of water.

"It's been over three years since the attack, Jules. And still the dreams come and go for no particular reason that we can see. It does sometimes seem hopeless."

"Well, I'm not going for hopeless. Yes, the dreams appear randomly, none for three months then two this week, but that's the point. Something has got to be setting them off. So come on, girlie. Get on with it. Step me through your scintillating day in the back office of Belmond's of London."

I sat up straighter and squeezed Jules' hand.

"Thanks, Jules. I know it's tough on you, too, having to keep going backward. You were as badly hurt as I was."

"Yeah, but I don't get it all back in glorious technicolor when I'm asleep. So, yesterday, you got up, showered and walked to the bus stop. Take it from there."

I closed my eyes to concentrate and talked Jules through my very ordinary day. The queue at the bus stop, the passengers on the bus, a day at work in the office and we searched for a something — a pair of eyes that reminded me, a certain chunky body shape, beer on none-too-fresh breath, a piece of jewelry that looked similar to that taken from us — and came up with nothing, as usual. Jules put her arm around my shoulders when I finished.

"The trouble is that we've got so little to go on. It was so dark and once we were both down, we were in too much pain to take in the detail. But we're not giving up, Ness. We'll work it out one day."

I slipped my arm around my friend's waist.

"I hope so, because one thing I'm sure of is that I'm never going back on those tranquillizers the doctor gave me, even if I have to be like this until I'm old enough that I don't remember the bad stuff because my memory has leaked out through my ears."

Jules wrinkled her nose. "It was a bit like living with an automated puppet, babe. But the police have still got the DNA from under our fingernails. It'll make it better for both of us if they catch up with them one day."

I sniffed and rubbed my finger under my nose. "At least nobody will take us down like that again."

Jules sat up straighter. "Too right they won't. The Girls' Club has made sure of that. Anyone tries sneaking up on us like that and they're going to be the ones eating dirt, not us."

I let go of Jules' waist, picked up my phone and checked the time.

"It's nearly five. I'll try and get a couple more hours' sleep. If I go into work already yawning, I'll have nodded off at my desk even before the first coffee run at ten."

"Why don't you just tell the agency you'd prefer something else?"

I shook my head. "No, I'll have to see the rest of the six-month contract through at Belmond's. It'll look bad on my resume if I change jobs too quickly, although I could kill Liz at the agency. A challenging position in the finance department is what I asked for. A data entry payroll clerk is what I got."

Jules smiled and swung her legs off the bed.

"Yep, stunning use of your degree there, girlie. But you've nearly got the first month out of the way and at least you've got the Maisie, Annie, Jason thing to watch to stop you from falling asleep."

I slid down the bed and flicked my duvet over my legs.

"Well, Maisie was definitely the winner today by two coffees to one. And it's the big day tomorrow. The solid wall is coming down and the new half-glass one's going in."

I blew Jules a kiss as she turned my light out.

"Thanks, Jules."

"Night, Ness. See you in a couple of hours."

Home of Erotic Romance

Sign up for our newsletter and find out about all our romance book releases, eBook sales and promotions, sneak peeks and FREE romance books!

About the Author

I love:
Being with family and friends.
Writing and having the freedom to do so now child four of four has passed her driving test and is off to uni later this year.

I Like:
Any excuse to throw a party.
Any excuse to open a bottle of fizz.
Shoes in vast quantities — the higher the heel the better.

Ambitions:
To write many more books.
To own a pair of Louboutin's.
To never go near an iron or a hoover again.

Cassie loves to hear from readers. You can find her contact information, website details and author profile page at https://www.totallybound.com

Printed in Great Britain
by Amazon